ROMESH GUNESEKERA

REEF

GRANTA BOOKS
LONDON
in association with
PENGUIN BOOKS

GRANTA BOOKS

2–3 Hanover Yard, Noel Road, London N1 8BE

Published in association with the Penguin Group
Penguin Books Ltd, 27 Wrights Lane, London W8 5TZ, England
Viking Penguin, a division of Penguin Books USA Inc.,
375 Hudson Street, New York NY 10014, USA
Penguin Books Australia Ltd, Ringwood, Victoria, Australia
Penguin Books Canada Ltd, 10 Alcorn Avenue,
Toronto, Ontario, Canada M4V 3B2
Penguin Books (NZ) Ltd, 182–190 Wairau Road,
Auckland 10, New Zealand

Penguin Books Ltd, Registered Offices: Harmondsworth,
Middlesex, England

First published in Great Britain by Granta Books 1994
This edition published by Granta Books 1995

3 5 7 9 10 8 6 4 2

Printed in Great Britain by Clays Ltd, St Ives plc

Helen

I am grateful to the Arts Council of Great Britain for a Writer's Bursary, and the British Library for its research facilities.

My special thanks to those who helped me individually in so many ways, both there and here, to discover and to write.

Of his bones are coral made

The Tempest

Contents

The Breach   11

I   Kolla   15

II   Cook's Joy   55

III   A Thousand Fingers   113

IV   Strandline   181

The Breach

AT THE PETROL station the forecourt was empty except for my car, an old red Volkswagen that used to be Mister Salgado's. I unlocked the tank and filled it right to the top as he had taught me to. Thick fumes rose in the cold night air. Then I wrote down the mileage, the volume, the date in a little logbook and went up to the cashier to pay.

The door was locked but someone's face peeped from behind the reinforced service window; almost a reflection of my own. I asked him whether he was from Sri Lanka. He smiled sheepishly and nodded. I passed my money over and he punched the keys of his electronic till. Nothing happened. He hit the side of the machine and smiled again at me. 'Wait, wait,' he said. He banged it again and looked under his counter.

I asked what was wrong.

He shook his head. He swept aside some papers and pushed the till. It didn't budge. 'One minute,' he said. 'Wait!' He moved back and picked up a telephone. There were some numbers written on a card stuck to the wall next to it. But then he looked over his shoulder at me and shoved the phone back.

I told him to turn the key on the machine. There must be a way. I tried speaking in Sinhala, but he shook his head. Wrong language. 'Tamil, Tamil. English only little,' he said. The tip of his tongue hovered.

'Sir, come inside, please.' He hurried to the door and unlocked it. 'Please. Please.'

I went in.

He led the way to his cubicle. Lifting the hinged counter top, he sat me next to the till. 'My first night,' he said. He picked up the telephone again. 'You speak, please.'

'Who to?'

'Boss. Won't understand. You speak, please. You know, please.' He pointed at the till and shrugged. He switched off the lights outside. Even so cars turned in and out with their headlights arcing through the window like searchlights. He would duck every time.

'How long have you been here? In this country?' I asked.

'Very bad war now back there. My home up by Silavatturai, you know?' He smiled eagerly.

I could see a sea of pearls. Once a diver's paradise. Now a landmark for gunrunners in a battle zone of army camps and Tigers.

'You live close by?' he asked hopefully.

I told him I had a business nearby, a restaurant.

He sucked in a jet of freezing air. 'You in this country a long, long time then?'

I nodded. More than twenty years now. A long time protected from the past.

'Starting with nothing?' He asked as if by saying it he would make it true. He too was painting a dream.

A drunk stumbled towards us in the dark. He started

hammering on the window. My every breath seemed imbued with petrol. I wanted to close my eyes and imagine a warm sea and our salt in the air. I did not know what I was doing in there. I and my young refugee with his flickering cash register. He clicked another switch and the cubicle light went out. Then, as the stars brightened, I remembered a bay-fronted house six thousand miles away.

I

KOLLA

'MISTER SALGADO IS a real gentleman. You must do whatever the hell he tells you.' My uncle pulled my ear. 'You understand, *kolla?* Just do it.' I was eleven years old. It was 1962: the year of the bungled coup. My uncle was escorting me to a house in a town I had never been to before.

The two columns at the front of the house plunged into beds of scarlet *rathmal* and white jasmine. The big bay between them, and the front windows, were shielded by cane tats painted in mildewy green. They were skew-whiff, unthreaded in places and splattered with bird-droppings. The roof was a line of reddish clay curls. A colossal white tree with tiny flecks of flame presided over the garden.

My uncle took me into the back of the house through a side entrance.

Inside, a door with a long grey metal spring attached to it squeaked behind us, closing automatically. A crumpled old woman was sitting on a small wooden stool with her feet in the sun. She looked up. 'You are back again?' she said to my uncle. 'What is this coming and going so much?' Her mouth collapsed around her empty gums.

My uncle told her we were there to see Mister Salgado.

She got up, wincing, and slowly made her way into the main part of the house. 'I will ask,' she mumbled.

We sat on the floor and waited. My ear hurt from my uncle's tug. When the sun sank behind the rooftops, we were summoned: *'Ko?'* a voice called from somewhere deep inside the house. *Where?* The polished syllable echoed. The last rays of light splintered through the trees. My uncle pushed me forward, 'Let's go.'

At first Mister Salgado said nothing. My uncle too was a man of few words. They were both silent for a while, simply wagging their heads at each other like puppets in the air. Eventually Mister Salgado nodded towards me: 'So, this is the boy?'

'Yes, this is the boy.' My uncle shifted his weight from one foot to the other, leaning towards the wall. One hand groped for support, the other proffered a bag of green mangoes we had brought. To him, Mister Salgado was probably not much more than a boy, but a boy whom history had favoured—a product of modern feudalism— whereas my uncle was a road-runner, a driver for an oil company. 'This is the one I was telling about. He is the boy. He can learn very quickly.'

A smooth untroubled face stared at me. 'School? Did you go?'

'Yes,' I blurted out. 'I went to school. Fifth Standard. I can read and write.' I had even learned some English from my poor, tormented schoolmaster, still under the spell of a junglified Victoria. He lived in a limewashed bungalow near my father's fields.

'And now?'

My uncle wriggled next to me. 'As I told before, he can learn quickly but he cannot live at home any more. That trouble . . .'

I had burned the thatched roof of a hut in the schoolyard by accident. I only dropped a single match flaring down the mouth of my father's almost-empty arrack bottle: a whistle of blue flame shot out and climbed the *cadjan* fronds. My father went mad; I ran away to my uncle who promised to arrange a new life for me. He told me I would never have to go back again. 'I am doing this only because I think your mother—if she were alive—would have wanted me to. Understand?'

Mister Salgado sighed. He was thin and had a curved spine. He often twisted himself into the most awkward postures, his long legs intertwined and his neck alarmingly cricked. The sad expression of a hurt heron would struggle in his face. He spoke slowly, almost hesitantly, politely changing the subject and asking my uncle about the failed coup as if it were some unseasonable rain. I had never heard language so gently spoken. My uncle's speech, in comparison, was a strangulation of the spirit. Ever after, when Mister Salgado spoke, I would be captivated. I could lose myself in his voice; this happened not only on that first day, but frequently over many years. Sometimes I would miss the instructions he was trying to give me, but he didn't always notice. I think he himself was sometimes entranced by his voice and lost the sense of what he had started out to convey. Perhaps that was why he sometimes preferred to be silent. I could understand that. My head also sometimes seemed more full of words than could ever pass my lips.

*

MISTER SALGADO, Ranjan Salgado, was a bachelor. A sweet smell clung to him, heady and unnatural, derived from an ivory bottle shaped like a bell and impossible to open properly. He would shake tiny, powerful drops out of the metal clasp at the top of its narrow neck and rub them on his hands, or his face or body. The scent made me think of cinnamon bushes, but it was the nature of the town to deceive. Even in Mister Salgado's house deceit had found a nest, especially in the head of his servant Joseph.

Mister Salgado would sit in his chair after his meal and rest his cheek, or his chin, or sometimes even his whole head on a thin finger or on a cupped palm—inviting misfortune—and stare with his huge eyes into nothing as if all he wanted was to grow old. He sat at the head of the dark mahogany table that I learned to polish to a deep and brilliant shine. At night, when alone, he usually liked to eat bread and western food: *courses*. Small discs of fried meat and creamy mashed potatoes that disappeared without a trace into his body. Corned beef was a favourite. He ate it with a *seeni-sambol* that burned the roof of your mouth. When, eventually, I became his cook as well as everything else, I created a special hash: crispy corned beef roasted with potatoes, onions and green chilli, dappled with soy sauce and brown sugar. I relished it too.

At first my job was simply to take the young master his morning tea and then sweep the front veranda and steps. Until I proved myself I was not allowed even to make tea, or dust or sweep inside the rooms. I was glad. I did not want to break anything.

The broom I was given was enormous. I was terrified that I would knock something over and so I would use the side door from the kitchen to go around the outside of the house to get to the front. I didn't dare go through the sitting-room or dining-room with it. One day I had a brilliant idea: I cut the handle short. That was the start of the trouble with Joseph.

'Stupid idiot, you chicken-head bumpkin, you pumpkin-face. Have you no respect for property? You are here to look after things, not destroy them.'

I was meant to help Joseph, but he resented me right from the beginning. Perhaps because, despite my circumstances, I was not of his kind. Joseph had come to work for Mister Salgado two years earlier. He was from Kosgahapola, a small brackish village on the other side of Ambalangoda beyond the mask-makers. He had wriggled his way into a job in a government Rest House until a by-election resulted in his being kicked out. The opposition had won, and the local party workers were being paid off, or at least that's what he had said to Lucy-*amma*, the very first person I had met in the house, Mister Salgado's cook-woman. More likely he was caught pilfering. Despite his high-horse ranting he could never hold back; he had been born with the moral equivalent of a sweet tooth—no temptation was too small. I despised him for this defect: I felt he sullied Mister Salgado's house.

But that day it was as though I were the one who had disfigured the place, as if the broom were some living creature I had dismembered, a scion of a dynasty instead of a wooden pole with a worn-out coir head. We never replaced brush-heads in that house until the bristles completely disappeared: it was a household trait. Mister Salgado, priding himself on his skills of measurement, never even replaced a toothbrush until there was practically nothing left but the plastic handle. I would watch the bristles get shorter and more squashed day after day, until sometimes I myself would go and buy him a new one and place it in his mug. I would hide the old one in the bathroom cabinet—I never quite had the courage to throw it out—but invariably it would appear again the next day in its usual place, unusurped. But I was right to cut the broom handle and Joseph was wrong to scold me. Our young master heard the commotion and came out of his room. Joseph complained vociferously but my Mister Salgado said, 'No, it's all right. The boy needs a shorter broom.' Then I knew I was in the right place; *he*, at least, did not think I was stupid.

*

JOSEPH LAID down the rules. He told me where I could sleep at night, 'Under that small, round hole'—a window in the alcove of the sitting-room—and what time I should get up. At night after he had turned out all the main lights and locked the front door, I would bolt the concertina doors in the sitting-room—one bolt into a dimple in the cold cement floor, the other into a cross-beam—and curl up on my mat under the porthole. I usually positioned myself so that I could look out while waiting for sleep to overcome me. I would imagine a star-chart in the sky that would cause the fall of Joseph—some terrible mishap, preferably preceded by disgrace before the master—and my own meteoric rise in the household. Early in my childhood I had convinced myself that I had a *deviya*'s divine ability to control my dreams, and so each night I would dream of revenge.

One night I decided to turn Joseph into a frog. I went to sleep sweet with anticipation. But in the middle of the night I woke up in a sweat. Something had gone wrong. I could not move. I was locked into position, petrified. My heart was pounding: a demon had entered the house. I prayed for it to go away and promised to be good and obey everyone around me and worship the god of all the gods if only the monster would go. Hours later, or minutes later, when there had been no sound inside the room, I began to feel brave again. I rolled off the mat and jumped to my feet. Nothing happened. No dagger flashed down; no demon pounced. There was no one to wrestle, only my own shadow from the half-moon and the scuttle of a startled gecko. I crouched and waited. Slowly as I realized that there really was no one there I began to play a game where all kinds of marauders entered the house and I, alone, repelled them. But in the end all that happened was that I overslept. When I opened my eyes it was morning. Joseph was nudging me with his foot. 'Get up,' he was saying. 'Get up, you stupid bastard.' The blue-and-white Chinese vase floating on the dark sideboard shook. I thought it was going to fall and break. But it was I—my body—that was shaking, not the vase. I rolled away again but without the energy I had had in the middle of the night. Sleep had wasted me.

'Tea! Tea!' Joseph was furious. 'Take tea to master. Get up, you lazy cow, take the tea!'

Fumbling with my sarong, I struggled to my feet. I could not stop rubbing my eyes. Without a word I rushed to the kitchen. Lucy-*amma* had put the tea to brew and even got the tray out for me. I quickly wiped the cup with the edge of my sarong and poured the tea. Milk and half a spoonful of sugar. It had always been that: just enough milk to turn the clear brown into creamy mud, and half a teaspoon of white sugar to fortify it. I knotted my sarong again, tight, and took the tea in.

Mister Salgado was in bed snoring lightly in the heat. The over-sheet was crumpled up on a side, and his sarong lay sloughed off his slim hips. His banyan revealed a few strands of black hair on a narrow boyish chest.

I went in and placed the tray on the side-table, 'Sir, tea!'

He was awake but he kept his eyes closed. He pretended to be asleep so that he did not have to acknowledge me. Early in the morning he was always very particular about maintaining his privacy. His *Einstein-time*, as he would call it later in life. I had learned that he liked me to leave the tea and disappear without a word. Then he would get out of bed and go to the chair by the window to sip his tea as if he were never comfortable in his large, dreamily soft bed with its padding and coir and coiled springs. But this morning I stayed on. I felt guilty for being late; I also wanted to do something to protect my standing from the criticisms that I knew Joseph would make later in the morning.

'Sir,' I declared, 'last night someone tried to break into the house. Sir, I chased them away, really . . . '

He groaned softly and turned. The bed creaked under him. On the headboard a small lamp rocked. I felt the whole room turn with his movement. He was tall, and when he was lying down he seemed to go on forever. His feet stuck out over the end of the bed, uncovered; he had high insteps that seemed to bunch his toes and shorten his feet. They looked like the feet of a woman.

'Sir, might have been *thieves*.'

I could see only half his face; one side was buried in the pillow. He opened an enormous brown eye and stared at me. A bare shoulder rose and dropped with each warm breath. Two inoculation scars like patched-up bullet holes flattened the skin of his upper arm. His sleep seemed luxurious. He made a sound like a hum, an all-purpose grunt. It was not a question, neither was it a statement, but it acknowledged my existence and the fact that I had said my piece. The dark, dreamy eye slowly closed, the pupil furling fast; the audience was over.

*

'WHAT HAPPENED?' Joseph asked when I got back.

'Nothing,' I said. 'I gave the tea.'

'Still asleep?'

I deliberately did not answer. Let him imagine the worst, the worst for him. It made my blood boil just to think of him contaminating the world with his foul breath, controlling my destiny. I turned my head as if I were hiding something and ducked into the kitchen.

Lucy-*amma* was cutting onions, Bombay onions. The beards sliced off each onion were heaped on one side. She worked the knife like a stern goddess—a *devatara*—slicing translucent, perfect semicircles. She was always cutting onions. I learned something from that: the omnipresence of the onion, constantly appearing like the heart's throb of our kitchen life. For breakfast, for lunch, for dinner, for every meal it turned up: sliced or chopped.

I learned about cutting onions mostly by watching Lucy-*amma*, but she also taught me by getting me to do it. I became her kitchen assistant—an apprentice onion-cutter. I was grateful for that role even though at first, I suppose because I was young and small and near to the cutting-surface, I would weep as I did it. I could do nothing about that except grow older and taller. Only much later did I learn the tricks to minimize the effects: like washing the onion, sticking bread on the tip of the knife, winding a damp cloth around my hand. But even now, most of the time I still do none of these: I just cut, crying cathartically.

In those early days my interest in onions had nothing to do with my ambition to be a cook. It started as a refuge; an escape from Joseph. He could not stand the fumes of a good strong onion. When we were cutting onions, and especially when we were frying them, he did not come anywhere near the kitchen. He would flee to the bottom of the garden. I became more and more embroiled in cooking onions simply to avoid him.

That morning, after my late start, I found Lucy-*amma* chopping at high speed with her eyes half-closed. She had been cooking since the turn of the century. The place where she had been born had turned from village to jungle and back to village, time and again, over her seventy-odd years. The whole country had been turned from jungle to paradise to jungle again, as it has been even more barbarically in my own life. Some nights I would sit on the floor beside her and listen to stories of the old days. She had known Mister Salgado as a child while she was bringing up her own, and his father as a child when she was one. She had served Mister Salgado's grandfather whisky and coffee during the riots of 1915. She had seen politicians with handlebar moustaches and tortoiseshell topknots, morning coats and gold-thread sarongs, barefoot and church-shod. She had seen monkey-suits give way to Nehru shirts; Sheffield silver replaced by coconut spoons. But her cooking and her wood-stove—two black stones outside the kitchen—remained timeless. The rice still took twenty minutes to cook, and if the lid was lifted before the dimples appeared all would be lost; and, she explained, you still could not tell a fresh coconut without shaking it, and you could not make a *pol-sambol* without breaking it. Culinary taste was not fickle, she would say, and the way you swallow food, like the way you make babies, has not changed throughout the history of mankind.

'You need this one?' I asked, picking up a small red onion. The dry papery skin crackled. She did not answer.

Her eyes were half-closed, protected against the vapours; her knife was a blur of steel.

I took the onion and cut it in half, and then neatly cut each half in half again. It was a small onion and the quarters fitted in the hollow of my hand; rattling, in a muffled sort of way, like dice in a gambler's fist.

I was not entirely sure what I would do with the onion quarters, but I knew that I wanted to bring the two—the onion and Joseph—uncomfortably together.

*

MISTER SALGADO'S house was the centre of the universe, and everything in the world took place within its enclosure. Even the sun seemed to rise out of the garage and sleep behind the *del* tree at night. Red-beaked parrots and yellow-eared *salaleenas* came and sang in the garden. Bullfrogs croaked by the gate. On Monday the greengrocer turned up with his basket of okra and beans; on Tuesday the butcher with oxtail and a hunk of goat-meat; on Wednesday the fishmonger came balancing sprats and prawns in two baskets on a pole calling out,

> *Isso, isso,*
> *thora malu,*
> *para malu,*
> *ku-nis-so-o.*

And on Thursday the haberdasher appeared with a cardboard trunk on his head. There was no point in his coming to our house—he sold only to women and the only woman in our house was Lucy-*amma* who never even looked at what he had to offer. But the man was a friend of Joseph and he came to gossip. His lips were splayed out, permanently parted, as if continuously spewing a web of intrigue.

He was due at mid-morning. I decided to wait for his arrival because Joseph would chat to him for at least half an hour and that would give me time to get into his room with my raw onion and do something diabolical: rub onion juice all over his sleeping-mat. Until then I busied myself on the front veranda, sweeping dust from one end to the other and into the garden, making a cloud of red motes puff out of my broom head.

The haberdasher had a little handbell which he rang as

he criss-crossed his way down the lane. Each time he rang the bell the crows on the road scrambled into the air. The whole place echoed with their cawing, his tinkling and the cooing of our neighbour's brainless doves. It was the march of a wizard. There was a house on the other side of our lane where he always stopped: number eight, Mr Pando's house. It was a mysterious fortress with high walls. From the lane nothing could be seen of the house except the edge of the roof; the haberdasher always got in but I never did, even though years later we got to know Mr Pando quite well. The tinkling of the bell would suddenly stop and there would be silence punctuated by the occasional shrill exclamation of Mrs Pando—the *nona*—discovering gold brocade, or the price of a fake emerald bangle. But this morning when he stopped outside the barricade and the tinkling died there was something missing. The massive door in the wall did not ease open: the whole lane tensed up. Then to my surprise the bell began to tinkle again. At first rather tentatively, as if the ringer were unsure as to what he should do. Then more insistently, as if he were trying to force the door open with the peals of his tiny bell. It was furious enough to wake the dead, but there was no response from number eight. He shouted out '*badu badu badu* . . .' goods and goodies, and then his voice trailed into a kind of puzzled anxiety. No sale at number eight today. He rang his bell slightly less enthusiastically and came towards our house.

'So, so?' I heard Joseph say to the vendor when he appeared. He was leaning over the gate, swinging to and fro.

'Those people must have gone somewhere.'

'Can't be. I heard them earlier in the morning. Big commotion was going on there with that Pando-*nona*.'

I had heard it too but had taken no notice. Joseph wiped his face with a corner of his sarong and waved the haberdasher in. His friend was a stocky man whose dark, round face was always dripping with sweat. When he squatted and eased the cardboard trunk down, he looked like a toad. The top of his head was flat and disfigured without the huge trunk on it. The flatness came from a cloth ring he wore on his head as a cushion. He took that off too and fanned himself, slowly rocking back and forth on his haunches. 'She even asked me to bring lace today.' He snapped open the brassy locks of the trunk and poked at a bundle inside. 'And look, georgette.' He cleared his ugly throat.

'What she want lace for?'

'Same as anybody. Why not? What do you think she wants?'

Joseph sniggered.

I turned to go to Joseph's room, but suddenly there was the most terrible howl I had ever heard: starting as a rumble in the bowels of the earth it erupted somewhere beyond the garden, filling the air with pain and fury; a bestial sound, demonic in its anguish like the screech of some gut-roasted bird, or the squeal of a punctured pig; a sickly sound stretched by a rack and wound around the boreholes of a drill, searing the nerve-ends of every jellified maggoty head in the neighbourhood. This was a howl loud enough to dwarf the history of sound in our lane, maybe the whole town, even the whole country.

Joseph and his friend ran out into the middle of the lane. I darted back into the garden. We all looked at Mr Pando's house: the source of the howl. Someone—a woman—started shouting. Doors banged. Glass shattered.

More screaming and screeching. I climbed to the top of the white tree in the front garden.

The whole of Mr Pando's front yard had turned powdery red as if covered with dust from Mars. The steps were strewn with small plastic bags. A woman hurried out and swept the powder off the steps. Then there was another howl from the house and she scampered back inside. There was more shouting, voices rising higher and higher. The crows were distraught, cawing and circling above the house. The sky turned black. Pando-*nona* rushed out and looked at the sky, and then rushed back in swearing. The howling carried on in huge, long, unearthly moans, rising and falling to a rhythm of its own.

Joseph and his friend and all our other neighbours gathered outside the house. The haberdasher was the one, in the end, who went in after the police smashed the door down.

When he came back he was hopping up and down. '*Miris, machang*—chillies! Those two witches tried to kill Pando-*mahathaya* with chillies. Hot, dry, red chillies and chilli powder. Place is covered all over with it.' His face streamed with sweat, his eyes brightened over every word. 'Pando-*mahathaya* was tied up in the bath. To see him, *appo!*' he banged the side of his head. 'His face, his arms, his balls, even his prick, all swollen like balloons. *Big*, man. They'd rubbed chilli powder all over. He was howling in agony. *Nona*-lady was screaming at him and pouring buckets of chilli powder. And that servant woman was rubbing it in. Up his arse!' Our witness laughed, prodding himself with his finger and wriggling about.

When the police dragged the two women out, Pando-*nona* was still screaming at her husband. 'I'll give you the hots, you *bathala*-poker.' It seemed she had discovered her recently-wed husband frolicking in the bathroom with a girl from the famous Hothouse Bodega. His howling and her screaming ring-marked everything in the whole neighbourhood: stones, trees, buildings, people. Poor Pando's skin retained a reddish tinge ever after, and he was always mopping himself with a big white handkerchief as if he were permanently too hot.

I went back into the kitchen and chucked my onion quarters into a bowl; they seemed too tame, but I was not ready to use chilli yet.

*

THE NEXT year, in September, Mister Salgado had planned
to go away for a few days to his cousin's tea-estate. Joseph
was to be left in charge of the house. I had to stay with
him as there was nowhere else for me to go. I had been in
the house for more than a year, but I was not happy. As
long as Joseph presided over me I could not be, and if I
stayed in that condition I knew, eventually, I too would
become corrupted and mean-spirited.

In preparation for Mister Salgado's absence, we closed
up the house and fitted white linen sheets over the furniture in the sitting-room and the dining-room. Joseph
supervised. I tugged and pulled and tucked and smoothed,
and turned the whole place into a funeral parlour. I was
given instructions on a huge new range of duties: polishing
the brass, the copper, the silver; oiling door hinges, locks,
pulley-wheels on the tats; making all kinds of inventories. I
had to count the cutlery, count the china, count the linen,
count the number of bulbs in the house, the books in the
bookcases. These counting jobs came straight from the
master himself. The night before he left, every time he saw
me, his eyes would widen and he would ask me to count
yet another thing. Catching sight of me down the corridor,
carrying out some earlier instruction such as taking the silver goblets to their treasure chest, he would say, 'Ah!' and
ensnare me with his voice. 'This . . . ' Everything would
stop. I would wait while he paused to clear his throat and
find the word he was looking for. 'Yes, I think you must
count all the different glasses we have. You must learn to
distinguish between the types, the shape you know, and
how many. Not now, but while I am away.' Then he would
lift his head questioningly like a teacher—a *gurunanse*.

'Yes, Sir.'

I had to go and write down all these different tasks. Early on I learned the value of making lists from watching Mister Salgado. He was a great one for lists. He would listen to *The Mikado* and write page after page of lists: shopping lists, laundry lists, book lists, betting lists, things-to-do lists, things-not-to-do lists, diary lists, repair lists, packing lists, record lists, larder lists, letters-to-write lists. I would find these on his desk, in the pockets of the clothes I had to put away, sometimes by the telephone and sometimes in his bag, like charms or favourite poems.

My lists, at that time, were always small ones: a scrap of paper—usually the one-inch margin of an old newspaper, torn from an inside page. I used to feel guilty about even that—my furtive attempts to emulate him and better myself—because the old newspapers in the house were sold to a collector who came once a month. My scraps for learning were a small loss in income for him. He came with a basket on his head and scales folded in a cloth in his hand. The newspapers were stacked in neat square piles and tied crosswise with dirty twine. Each bundle would be weighed and paid for. Then with a month's news neatly placed on top of his head, he would rise and waddle away. The knowledge that could be packed into that basket was humbling; everything that happened in the world for a whole month. Sometimes I would use an old envelope retrieved from the straw basket in the study. I would write my list with a pencil and keep it in my shirt pocket.

On the evening I was asked to count the glasses I was getting increasingly anxious; my list was becoming unwieldy. I liked to keep it neat, writing just on one side with careful, evenly spaced letters. It was the way I learned to write. I didn't like squeezing in words or adding a line where there really ought not to be one. And because newspapers were so thin, I didn't much like writing on both sides. I press too hard when I write and the other side of the paper tends to become embossed. I also do not like having more than one list—unlike Mister Salgado. But that night rushing about, listening for his awkward signals—his Ahs and Hmms, the pauses, the instructions—I ended up with too many things to do. If these were exercises to stimulate me, to develop skills of classification and mathematics, they were in danger of failing completely.

Although he had been to the best of Colombo's schools, Mister Salgado regarded himself as largely self-educated. He came from a line of people who believed in making their own future. To him there were no boundaries to knowledge. He studied mosquitoes, swamps, sea corals and the whole bloated universe, and right from the early days wrote long articles about all of them. He wrote about the legions under the sea, the transformation of water into rock—the cycle of light, plankton, coral and limestone—the yield of beach to ocean. I sometimes burst in on him in his study when, pen in hand, he was poised on the brink of some miraculous calculation. 'Sorry, Sir,' I would say and he would motion me to be quiet. 'Listen, do you know how many stars there are in the sky?' I would shake my head, 'No, Sir.' He would nod and smile to himself. 'They have been counted, you know, but nobody can count how many polypifers surround us in the sea.'

The morning he was due to leave for up-country I was allowed to serve breakfast. I brought him his plantain, his soft-boiled egg, his toast and butter and pineapple jam, in real trepidation. He was deep in thought. When I came to take his plate away, he looked up at the ceiling fan and spoke like a sage, 'You must look after this place.'

'Sir?' But before I could say anything else Joseph appeared, rubbing his head with the heel of his palm nervously. 'Everything ready, Sir.'

Later that morning Lucy-*amma* also went away, on her annual visit home. 'Now, make sure you eat some rice every day. Joseph will give you food. There is money in the biscuit tin to get something from the *kadé*,' she said, tying up her belongings in an old tablecloth.

'He won't, I know he won't.' I hated the idea of being dependent on him. 'He is jealous of me, he'll want me to starve.'

'Don't be stupid, child.'

I carried her bundle down to the gate. It smelled of boiled rice and coconut milk, just as she did. She lifted it up on top of her head like the paper-collector, the bottle-man, the haberdasher, and disappeared down our magic road. I felt trapped. Blood pounded in my head at the thought that there was nobody else in the house—in the world—except Joseph and me. I felt like running around and around the garden in a never-ending circle like a mad dog, spinning faster and faster so that Joseph would never catch me, but instead I waited at the gate, as far away as possible from the house, and rubbed my elephant-hair bracelet for good luck.

What I disliked most about Joseph was the power he had over me, the power to make me feel powerless. He was not a big man but he had a long rectangular head shaped like a devil-mask. His face was heavy and his lower jaw jutted out, making his head look detached from his body. A sullen heart compressed the muscles beneath the skin of his face in a permanent grimace. He had big hands that would appear out of nowhere. And as I was always trying to avoid him and never looked up at him, the sight of his hands suddenly on a doorknob or reaching for a cloth was terrifying. The hands, like the head, always seemed disembodied. I expected to find them around my throat one day. The nails were in good shape though; he took good care of his nails. I don't know where he learned to look after them, but maybe he too learned something from our Mister Salgado.

When the clouds came and I smelled rain loosening in the air, I headed back up to the house. I didn't know what else to do: he would be there somewhere, waiting, gloating.

The kitchen was in darkness. The small windows by the sink did not let in much light, and because the place was empty the other doors were closed. I didn't want to turn on the lights and attract attention to myself; instead I groped along the edge of the side-table until I got to the counter where Lucy-*amma* did her cutting. Underneath I found a small basket of red onions. I quickly bit one open and rubbed it all over my hands. Then I put it inside my shirt for my protection. If he was to come anywhere near me I would fling it in his face, or smear it all over him. It was not chilli powder, but it would keep him away. I had to be prepared for anything. I hid in the back. Our part of the house—the kitchen, the storeroom, Lucy's room, Joseph's room, the spaces between the servants' warren and the back veranda—was always full of junk: old battle-worn chairs, empty cargo boxes, a buckled cupboard jammed against the wall where I hid my few belongings, a blistered chrome refrigerator, bald brushes and rust-eaten dustpans, a mangled electric blender, a wireless with its face punched in and a big, blackened iron. All the leftovers of city living washed up like driftwood. But it was comfortable.

The rain fell in small pellets ripping the petals off the flowers in the garden. I imagined Joseph outside, pierced by the drops, drenched to the bone, catching a chill, pneumonia, something deadly: an illness of the mind. In each needle line of rain, I saw a message for him from the gods, my gods. I could see them in the sky crowded on a bamboo raft on a blue lake surrounded by rolling hills, holding silver spears and peering through peep-holes in the clouds, searching for Joseph, determined to destroy him.

'Here, eat this.' Joseph threw a ready-made packet of rice and curry on to the chair next to me. 'I will be out tonight.' I had not heard him come up behind me because of the noise of the rain. 'I'm going when the rain stops. You close the doors and keep guard. Sleep inside.'

Where he had to go I could not imagine, but I was overjoyed. I wished the rain would stop immediately: instead it poured down even harder. The sound rose to a crescendo. Water drilling into the ground. The gutters were spilling over and waves seemed to wash down the sides of the veranda; the drain had turned into a river. Joseph disappeared into his room, and I reversed my prayers; I tried to will the rain to stop. 'Give us a break: let him go, leave the house, then come down as hard as hard can so he will never ever return. Let him drown as he walks slurping in the rain with that spoony jaw of his.'

At nightfall the rain stopped. Joseph left wearing a stylish pink shirt. The first thing I did was tuck into my ricepacket; I was starving but I had not wanted to eat while he was around. I did not want to give him the satisfaction of seeing me drool over food that he provided, but drool I did. I had eaten nothing since early morning when Lucy-

Romesh Gunesekera

amma gave me some bread which I had with a bit of butter left over on a breakfast plate. I stuffed my face, fist over fist.

That night was the first time I stayed alone in the house: our big town house with its cane blinds, Formica surfaces and nylon mats. It was a dark house; the lights never quite reached everywhere even when they were all turned on. Even the biggest bulb, a huge clear globe in the dining-room, seemed to be overshadowed by the space it had to illuminate: the ceiling barely discernible and some of the corners, the oblongs of shadow behind pieces of boxy furniture, indistinct. I always felt the place was bigger than its form, that each room extended beyond what I could see, that the house itself extended beyond what I could know, as if each room had a shadow room which only shadows could enter and where secret rituals of peculiar sciences—oceanography, sexology—were practised.

I sat out on the front steps and checked through the list of things to do for my Mister Salgado. For the first time I felt at peace in the house. Not only because of the quietness inside, the quiet of an empty house, but also because of the knowledge that Joseph was not roaming about inside. Knowing that I would not bump into him around a dark corner. Or see him glowering under some light, smirking. Not having his presence spoiling my life.

In the end I didn't do any of the jobs I should have. I planned out what I needed to do but then drifted away, imagining life in the house forever without Joseph. I felt I could spend my life growing in the house, making something of myself. I had the feeling that my Mister Salgado would help me. I also felt, even then, that Mister Salgado could do better with just me by his side. Joseph was not

38

the man for him. Joseph should be stuck up some palm tree, high on *toddy*, keeping the demons happy like the rest of his people. He made the house seem awkward and unbalanced. I felt he wanted to abuse everything in Mister Salgado's house like a drunk who resented what he could not reach, especially the sobriety of those who could stand where he would fall. I felt I could change that; smooth the house and cultivate our lives to some fruition. Perfection even. It seemed possible in those days.

I felt safer than I had ever felt before in my life. The silhouettes of the trees and bushes in the garden, the glow in the sky from the gas lamps on the main road seemed mine and only mine, embellished by familiarity. I didn't know what happened much beyond our lane. I knew the *kadé*—the tea kiosk at the top of the road, a few shops at the junction, and I had been to the market, but the rest of the city—what it means to be in a city—was a mystery to me. I had no idea how much I did not know about the city—Mister Salgado's *sleepy town*—beyond the few roads I had seen. I could not imagine where Joseph had gone. Was it some place in the heart of Pettah? A brothel? A den in the harbour area? What kind of place? In those days we had no television, and I had not read any books about life in the town we lived in. Only the newspapers gave some inkling, but not enough to give shape or sense to the place. I read about brawls in taverns, drug trafficking; courtroom dramas about the price of onions; the Profumo scandal rocking England; but I could not visualize the lie of the land, the real geography of the city or the sea between countries. The few grainy black-and-white pictures in the newspapers formed a shadow world of petrified garlands, smiling stupefied politicians and gnomic sorcerers' boxes. I had no real opening to the outside world; only walls everywhere, sometimes painted, sometimes with frescos—people, narratives, icons—or a mural to fool me completely, but nothing real. I was trapped inside what I could see, what I could hear, what I could walk to without straying from my undefined boundaries, and in what I could remember from what I learned in my mud-walled school. My head was like a balloon that had only a few puffs of air in it. Not enough to float up in the sky; not helium but a sadder more mortal air that only allowed it to loll about bumping into chairs and footstools and sleep huddled on the floor. But at least it had not been completely deformed by the spite so prevalent in our surroundings, the whole of our world. 'The politics of envy is the master of all our industry,' Mister Salgado used to say to characterize the times and the tussle everywhere for power.

The next morning was the best I had woken to, ever. The sun warmed my face. There was no sound in the house. No one was shouting at me. No pounding of flour, no coconut-scraping, no onion-chopping. Nothing even from our neighbours, no radios, no slap and slurp of washing. No hawking and spitting. I opened my eyes and stayed still. I did not have to do anything for anyone. The house was completely and utterly empty. Delicious, complete cow-head nirvana. It was as if Joseph had never been there.

But inevitably he intruded into my thoughts. I imagined him in some despicable hole in the most wretched part of the city, devoured by sorcerers and thieves. Even murdered: some miracle whereby my wishes had been picked up by the spirits of the city and been executed by some other agent. Had I stumbled on a deadly mantra? An inadvertent curse? When by mid-morning I still had not seen him, I was jubilant. I was sure the gods had intervened on my behalf.

If Joseph was dead then everything was really up to me. There was only a day before Mister Salgado was due to come back and there was a lot to be done. I realized I had better finish all the jobs he had given me to prove myself the right and proper successor to Joseph. I started by polishing the silver. It was a big job: Mister Salgado had a teak canteen full of cutlery which had belonged to his grandfather. It served a dozen people and had been the bedrock of that generation's grander socializing. He also had cups and school trophies and a silver-plated jug. I laid everything out like a picnic on newspaper spread out underneath the frangipani in the garden and set to work. The polish was almost nourishing to inhale: a rich odour of fenugreek and red lentils. The liquid worked itself under my fingernails as I rubbed it on the metal, coating it in a powdery flaking white skin, and removed it all black on a rag, then a newspaper, then another cloth, polishing and rubbing, sweating, until the pieces shone like molten sun on the lawn. If only my master would come now he could see me doing so well with the things he wanted done. I would do anything for him, if only I could remain in the house on my own—without Joseph.

My life until then had been the same as the lives of all those who leave their unhappy homes, their squabbling families, their claustrophobic riverbank asylums, and break out into a clear world beckoning from beyond the edge of their dreams, there to make at least a moment sparkle like a star in the night. But with my Mister Salgado I thought I might find something more, something that would really change the world and make our lives worthwhile. I polished the silver, I counted the cutlery, I did everything he asked me to, wishing I could see Joseph's corpse. What colour would it be? Bloodless? Grey? Without all that water and stuffing inside, would it be like a collapsed and empty bag? Take the blood away, the stuff that seeps out, and the soul that must leave it like any other parasite, what's left—in the case of Joseph—must be pretty pointless: a shrunken leather pouch. Bone, cartilage, rotting flesh and blubber. I had never seen a corpse in its natural state. It was not common in our countryside in those days. Our barbarities were startling but domestic: the dismembering of an adulterous husband, drunken homicide; occasionally acid thrown in a fit of jealousy near the more urban areas where the community had no hold, or political privilege gave protection. But there were no death squads then, no thugs so callous in their killing that they felt no pleasure until they saw someone twitch against a succession of bullets. In my childhood no one dreamed of leaving a body to rot where it had been butchered, as people have had to learn to do more recently.

In the afternoon the sun was hotter than it had been for some time; I went back into the house. I sat in the front bay with the bamboo tats half rolled up. The floor in the house was cool except where the sun fell directly on it. The breeze blew over the low parapet walls and under the greenish tubes of the tats. The sound of the breeze passing was in itself cooling. It was our version of the water gardens that are found in more rarefied countries, or back in our own more refined archaeological past. In the shade, I watched ants crawling across a warm step; small black beetles scurrying across a wilderness; soldiers marching up into the hills and warriors from some heavenly bush paradise descending to protect the roots of a croton hedge. I remembered the coconut trees of my childhood, the sound of the breeze through the fronds. Simple, pure, deathless air.

Most of all I missed the closeness of the tank—the reservoir. The lapping of the dark water, flapping lotus leaves, the warm air rippling over it and the cormorants rising, the silent glide of a hornbill. And then those very still moments when the world would stop and only colour move like the blue breath of dawn lightening the sky, or the darkness of night misting the globe; a colour, a ray of curved light and nothing else. The water would be unbroken like a mirror, and the moon would gleam in it. At twilight when the forces of darkness and the forces of light were evenly matched and in balance there was nothing to fear. No demons, no troubles, no carrion. An elephant swaying to a music of its own. A perfect peace that seemed eternal even though the jungle might unleash its fury at any moment. The tank was a sea made safe by human imagination, a vast expanse of water that ensured the health of our bodies and our minds and soothed our graceless lives. The city lacked such water. Mister Salgado's house had no visible body of water except when it rained. But even the rain quickly ran off; within an hour the place would be baking. A tank or a river provided a place with a kind of majesty that I felt the house—we—needed. A year later I convinced him—the young *mahathaya*—to build a small pond, a tin tank, in a corner of the garden. But it was not a success. The idea was good, and he perked up when I described it. '*Nelum* flowers and lilies, some goldfish to look at in the evening.' He was happy. 'Right,' he said, 'put it in the corner near the jam tree.' The idea fired his imagination but when it came down to it he was all theory, no practice. I had to be the engineer even though I had no training. My mistake was in the positioning. The jam tree shed so much fruit that the pond was soon full of rotting berries and dead leaves. And the fruit bats came to it every night. The lily-pads were spattered with their droppings, and the water turned filthy. It became the breeding ground for a vicious strain of mosquito. They fed on me. Huge monsters with suckers like elephant trunks. But Mister Salgado found the whole thing increasingly interesting: especially the mosquitoes. He made a study of their development and wrote a paper about insects and bat-droppings. Later he expounded his theories to a small circle of students. 'The mosquito . . . ' he would say, and you would think he was invoking a god in heaven. I would cup my ears to catch every reverberation of each word he would utter. 'The mosquito is a much-neglected beast. If we fail to study it and simply rely on DDT, we do so at our peril.'

Peril . . . DDT . . . beast. It was poetry to me. He made even the drone of a mosquito, which he mimicked in his discourses, as sensuous as the hum of a hummingbird.

But that day, sitting alone on the floor of the front bay, I had no notion of the future. I did not really believe that Joseph was dead, or that my life would improve. I wanted it to and I convinced myself that if I acted as though these things had happened and were happening, then they truly would. That some mischievous little godling would intervene with a triple-pronged arrow and prick fate towards my desires. The garden shimmered and I could even see mirages of our jewelled river, maybe that small *takarang* tank that was to come—our pond—hovering on the hot driveway. I drifted away in the heat of the afternoon, swelling and stretching, overcoming my unease.

I was woken by a sound in the house. I thought it might be one of the cats. The neighbourhood was full of strays. They were mangy, full of fleas and disaffected spirits. And they chased the birds that made their homes with us. My argument against them was that they pissed all over our bushes. Once I found an orange tom in the study. I shouted at it, and instead of going out of the window it jumped for the door. The stupid cat almost knocked itself out because I had shut the door behind me when I had entered. I had my belt in my hand to crack like a whip, but all I had to do was pick the animal up by the scruff of its neck and fling it out. Its eyes flared, the slits widening in the topaz, and it spat and hissed and yowled but never came back.

The sitting-room was as I had left it earlier: a morgue of white-sheeted furniture. I went down the corridor to the bedrooms. Mister Salgado's bedroom door was closed. I opened it.

Joseph was by the mirror. His face was pallid; his red eyes bulged. He had unbuttoned his shirt and was rubbing Mister Salgado's cologne on his chest. Talcum powder had settled on the tabletop. He looked up and saw me across the room, reflected in the mirror. He hissed something under his breath and turned quickly around. He came towards me locking me with his gaze. I couldn't move. I swallowed and swallowed but my mouth was dry. I couldn't get anything to move from inside. Joseph had his mouth open and his tongue thickened between his teeth. I could see the spittle on his lips bubbling. He lunged forward and grabbed me. I lashed out with my hand. If I could hit his jaw his tongue would fall out, but his arms were like steel belts around me. He pushed me down on the big soft bed. He was on top of me, twice my size, squeezing the life out of me and the breath out of my chest. His fist digging in between my legs and punching a hole in me. The more I struggled, the stronger he became. I bit his arm, and he nearly broke my back. In the end I gave up and died. I let the life out of my body, and he froze. Then with one hand he undid his sarong and pulled at his dribbling warped prick. He looked down at it, and I slipped out from under him down on to the floor. He rolled over still holding himself. He was breathing hard; his body was pumping. I found a shoe under the bed and flung it at him. I wanted to scream but I couldn't. I had no voice. I jumped up and ran out of the house.

I wanted to keep running, all the way up to the shops at the junction. But I knew if I did that, and if Joseph didn't chase me, I would not know where he was. I would not know when I could go back. I stopped at the gate. Every breath I took seemed to be fire; everything inside me was charged up. But I could do nothing. I waited for him to appear.

Eventually he came down the driveway and let himself out. He disappeared down the lane. I followed him up to the main road and then along it towards the sea. I had never been up that way. A bus came by, and I lost him.

Back in the bedroom the bed had been straightened out, but not as well as it should have been. I could still smell him there.

That night I learned to identify every tiny sound of the dark. Every creak in the garden, every hum on the main road, every flap of every bat that screamed into the jam tree. I listened even though I knew that footsteps could hardly be heard on our hard driveway. I wished I had scattered newspapers or dry leaves all around the place, or set up trip-wires four inches above the ground and attached to a bell. But I had not. And I could not now in the dark when he could pounce again.

*

MISTER SALGADO parked his car under the porch and, putting his hand on the roof, hauled himself out. The car creaked as his weight shifted; the side tipped, and he unravelled his long legs. 'Where's Joseph?'

I said I did not know.

'Get him here.'

'He's not in the house, Sir.'

'What?'

I had not searched the house, but I was sure I would have sensed it if he had returned. 'He hasn't been here since yesterday.'

From the way Mister Salgado looked at me, I might have been talking gibberish. 'What do you mean, he hasn't been here?'

'He went somewhere, Sir. He didn't tell me anything.'

Mister Salgado's eyes narrowed, and a small vertical furrow appeared in his broad forehead sucking in the skin where his eyebrows met. 'Unload this then.' He opened the boot of the car. It was full of fruit and coconuts. 'Take all this . . . ' he waved his hand about, 'take it to the back.' He went inside the house deep in thought.

I wondered what he really knew about Joseph.

I took the smooth, polished, pinkish coconuts and a small carriage of plantains into the kitchen. His bag I took to his bedroom.

'Some tea, Sir? Shall I bring?'

He looked up at me as if I were a total stranger. Then something ignited in his head. 'Yes. Bring tea.'

It was strange being the only person around to look after him, but I knew what to do. Nobody had to tell me.

When I went back to him with the tea-tray, he asked me, 'So, where did Joseph go?'

48

'He went somewhere in a bus.'

'A bus came here?'

'No, Sir, on the main road. He went and got on one.'

'You went with him?'

'No, Sir, I saw him. I was going to the *kadé*.' I don't know why I lied, but sometimes I start saying the wrong thing and find I cannot stop. I wanted to tell him exactly what I had seen and what had happened. But the words were impossible to get out. I did not want to be tarnished by telling—by putting into words—what had gone on. It would have spoiled everything. We would have had Joseph between us forever. It was not what I wanted. It was better, I thought, to leave it untold. That way maybe the event would fade. It would disappear. Without words to sustain it, the past would die. But I was wrong. It does not go away; what has happened *has* happened. It hangs on the robes of the soul. Maybe putting it into words can trap it. Separate it. Afterwards maybe it can go in a box, like a letter, and be buried. Or maybe nothing can ever be buried. I felt tense thinking of what to say. There was no way I could tell him the truth, however much I wished.

Late in the afternoon I heard the metal hasp on the gate clang back on its heels. Joseph came up the driveway with a slight swagger. A flock of feeding birds scattered out of his way. Everything about him suggested defiance. He had a small parcel wrapped in newspaper tucked under his arm; his sarong was hitched up a few inches to let him stride like a *chandiya*.

The closer he got, the louder the crows cackled. I felt the wind blow towards the house, the branches of the big white tree bent towards us and the spirits of the garden gathered around.

I wanted to shout out that Joseph was here, but I did not need to: Mister Salgado was in the front bay watching him walk up.

'Where did you go?' I heard him ask.

'Pettah, Sir.'

Mister Salgado was standing on the step. One hand was up to his face, gripping his chin between two long curled fingers, the other hand supported his arm. He looked at Joseph silently for a moment. 'So, what did you get?'

'Nothing, Sir.'

'What is the parcel then?'

Joseph seemed a little unsteady. From the garden I could not see his face until he shrugged and turned away from Mister Salgado. Then I could see he was drunk. His eyes were shining.

'You'd better go,' Mister Salgado said quietly. So quietly that I barely heard him. Joseph probably didn't hear him at all—being drunk. But the tone of Mister Salgado's voice, the angle of his head, the look in his eyes made the message clear. He meant really go. *Clear out. Roll your mat and disappear.* Mister Salgado in his quiet undemonstrative sober way was giving our Joseph the push. He was fired. Joseph did not understand.

'You'd better be out of this house before dark. Take your things and go. I don't want to see you here again.' Mister Salgado turned and went back into the house. Before he disappeared he shoved a hand in his pocket and pulled out a roll of notes. He dropped it on the table next to him: one month's severance pay, Joseph's notice. The course of Joseph's life had changed with those three short sentences. He looked like a buffalo whose head had been severed with one stroke of a Kali sword: it was dead but the head had yet to fall, a microsecond of illusion and reality conjoined. Alive and dead. Time melted, dripping with every breath he took.

I felt sorry for Joseph even though I hated him; the moment he began to fail, my feelings began to change. Like when you are pushing hard against a stubborn door which suddenly opens and gives way, and you have to pull back, just to regain your balance and not go falling headlong into nothing. I felt like that with Joseph. With those few quiet words, barely audible, Mister Salgado had reversed everything in our world. Not just for Joseph but for me too. We would undergo a revolution. In the light of this knowledge Joseph seemed to change in front of my eyes from a spumy barrel full of stunted frogs into a pitiful little man obsessed by the small world that he had lorded over and was now too stinking drunk even to understand what was happening to it. Eventually he scratched his ear, picked up the money and shuffled off towards our part of the house. He hardly noticed me.

Joseph had developed his taste for numbness, I think, smoking cigarette butts and draining the dregs of beer and liquor left by visitors to the Rest House where he worked before he came to Mister Salgado. He was the type who could dilute the bottle even as he poured the shots. But he didn't know what his limitations were; he thought just because he knew the habits of his superiors he could become one. It was his frustration, knowing there was no future for the likes of him in the kind of service he dreamed of, that turned him into a monster. The dream just ate him up: first the brain, then the eyes, the throat, then the prick. As he grew older he grew thicker-skinned until he was all bone and meat: there was no space inside for a conscience, for morality, for any inner life. He grew into a numbskull, a stupid monster. Malign spirits wormed into his heart. My Mister Salgado was too innocent to understand, but that day at least he had a glimmering and intuitively knew what he had to do.

I didn't say a word to Joseph. He went to his room and I heard him pack his things. A little later he went back into the house. I could hear him talking to Mister Salgado; I couldn't make out the words. Mister Salgado didn't seem to say anything in return. When Joseph came back out, he spat at my feet. 'You bastards, you are going to eat shit one day, shit.' He turned and disappeared, cursing the house, swearing to bury monkey skulls and pig entrails in our garden.

Mister Salgado called for me later that night. He was going out to eat; Lucy-*amma* had not returned yet. He asked me whether Joseph had gone.

'Yes, Sir,' I said. 'Took all his things and went.'

'He will not be coming back.' Mister Salgado looked at me. 'Can you do everything?'

I nodded, not even knowing what he meant, except that my dream was coming true.

'You will see to the whole house then.'

I felt overwhelmed by the responsibility. 'Sir, don't know how to do *everything*. May need *some* help.'

He lowered his head and let his voice envelop us both. 'Lucy will cook, but you'd better learn from her,' he said. 'You will have no problem learning. I can see that. You are a smart *kolla*. Really, you should go to school . . . '

'No, Sir.' I was sure, at that time, that there was nothing a crowded, bewildering school could offer me that I could not find in his gracious house. 'All I have to do is watch you, Sir. Watch what you do. That way I can really learn.'

He sighed, slowly releasing us into the future. 'Let's see.'

So I watched him, I watched him unendingly, all the time, and learned to become what I am.

II

COOK'S JOY

ALL OVER THE globe revolutions erupted, dominoes tottered and guerrilla war came of age; the world's first woman prime minister—Mrs Bandaranaike—lost her spectacular premiership on our small island, and I learned the art of good housekeeping.

Sam-Li, at number five, showed me how to stir-fry and turn a spring onion into a floating flower. Next door, Dr Balasingham's young son, Ravi, obsessed by the American Wild West, educated me in the history of the Apaches in his father's backyard. He would yell, *Geronimo!* and shoot the arrows I tipped with flattened nails, fletched with *bulbul* feathers. Once he got me in the head: a good quarter-inch of nail into my skull making a hole I can still feel in moments of stress. In return for my playing dead and other minor exorcisms, he let me devour his school primers and English readers. He had a private *guru* whom he aped, scratching his groin and scolding me for my rice-eating dimness while extolling the virtues of the brighter parrots and clip-winged mynah birds caged in his house. It didn't bother me; I was getting more than he thought out of our encounters.

The haberdasher stopped coming after Joseph left, but the other vendors continued to ply their trade at the gate and, in time, learned to treat me as the one who ran the place. Lucy-*amma* had retired back to her now-sprawling conurbation in the jungle. I parted my hair in the middle and grew in spurts, marvelling at the magic of my break in the house.

Mister Salgado's closest friend was Mr Dias Liyanage. He had known him from his schooldays. Dias had become a government officer, following in his father's footsteps, after varsity. His father had been involved in the programme for the Queen when she first came from England, and Dias often claimed that he spoke to her and travelled with her all the way to Polonnaruwa in his shorts. He told a lot of stories that made Mister Salgado laugh in his quiet way. 'But Dias,' he would tease, 'you must have been doing your matric by then!' Dias would look startled. 'What? No, no, no.' He would pause and then admit, 'All right, so I was sixteen and already in bloody college longs.' He would extend his neck out of his collar, like a tortoise, and wiggle his head as he cleared another tall story in his throat.

One evening he came over with a big buff folder under his arm. It was tied tightly with a red ribbon. 'Triton, where is he?' Mister Salgado was in his study. I went and called him. 'So, how?' Dias said, when he ambled into the room. 'Have you heard anything yet?'

'How about a drink first?'

'Just one, then. OK.'

I brought an ice-cold bottle of beer and poured two tall glasses to the brim.

Dias gave me a broad smile, 'Nice and cold huh, Triton? Very good, very good.' He drew on his cigarette and took a long sip. 'Ah, *wonderful*. So, have the buggers said anything about the project yet? Is there a job? Or is this Foundation of yours waiting to see which way the wind will blow?' His shoulders shook as he laughed and his head bounced all over like a punchball, releasing small puffs of cigarette smoke. He had a hiccupy laugh which broke out of him with increasing frequency when he was with Mister Salgado. He was always jolly, our dear Dias-*mahathaya*. Very different from Mister Salgado. He was physically smaller, but because he talked a lot and was so effervescent he seemed to fill up more space. He would smoke constantly and a froth of high-pitched words, burbles and, it has to be said, uncontrollable smoky burps bubbled out of him. His friends found this endearing and sometimes called him 'Andrews', after the liver salts they purged themselves with after a weekend binge.

'You won't believe it but I did a little boat trip last week, in Hikkaduwa. A glass-bottomed job. It's incredible, like you say, all that stuff underwater. Gave me vertigo, just looking. I didn't realize there were so many fantastic shapes. Some of these fish are something else, no?'

Mister Salgado nodded. 'We must go further south,' he said. 'Past Galle it's out of this world. Fabulous. But it's all going. I must take you before it all vanishes.'

'I brought you some papers our Fisheries people have produced. They also talk about this coral business.'

Mister Salgado undid the big loopy knot and opened the file. He flicked over the pages. 'You see, surveys have been done since the 1880s, but I don't think they have any real understanding of what is happening. Coral grows about as fast as your fingernails, but how fast is it disappearing? Nobody knows!'

'What, from dynamiting and all?'

'Anything! Bombing, mining, netting.' Mister Salgado dropped the file on the side-table. 'You see, this polyp is really very delicate. It has survived aeons, but even a small change in the *immediate* environment—even *su* if you pee on the reef—could kill it. Then the whole thing will go. And if the structure is destroyed, the sea will rush in. The sand will go. The beach will disappear. That is my hypothesis. You see, it is only the skin of the reef that is alive. It is real flesh: *immortal.* Self-renewing.' Mister Salgado threw up his hands, 'But who cares?'

'That is why they need you, *men*: the Foundation. Even Government. The Ministry. Otherwise some dingo will just make a pig's breakfast out of it.' Dias lit another cigarette from the glowing butt of his earlier one. 'Pig's breakfast, hey! Good one, no?'

'They say they have some funds, but I am still in two minds about it.'

'Don't be silly, Ranjan. You have to do it. After all those papers and all, and the letter you wrote that *gonbass* minister. You owe it to the country, what *men*? You can't just *hook* it now.'

Mister Salgado leaned back in his chair and rubbed his lips with two fingers held together, extended, as if remotesensing the inner contours of his mouth. 'But you know, if this thing becomes anything, some political bigwig will want his fat hands on it. Then every day I'll be asking for favours and doing favours. I will spend my whole life cajoling and coddling. Sucking and preening, breaking coconuts, cutting rice, patronaging all over the place.

Why would I want to do that? I don't want to feel *obliged* to anyone. I can live without that.'

'Nonsense, *men*. Those fellows have their own problems. What with the devaluation last year, and now this district council palaver, what do you think? All they want are some success stories. To show this country is finally joining the twentieth century. A Land-Rover, some hefty report. Politics, no? That's all.'

'You know, I am only an amateur in this. It's just that nobody knows any better.'

'That's it. That's just it.'

'I have to think about it some more.'

'Sometimes Ranjan, you think too bloody much for your own good.'

They had got to the end of their beers, and Mister Salgado would soon want to renew himself and Mr Dias on another bottle and then a plate of steaming string-hoppers laced with a red-hot fish curry.

I had become an expert in the kitchen. Although I used my hand as a spatula frying fish-balls in hot oil, the middle joint of my right little finger was as sensitive as a tube of mercury in judging the right temperature for a perfect string-hopper dough. I was also pretty good at a curry in a hurry. A nice red salmon dish could be on the table in twelve minutes flat, and they would both love it.

The flour was damp that night and had to be roasted on a metal tray before being sieved. I was collecting it in a newspaper cone when Mister Salgado came in. He asked me what I was doing. I said I was preparing string-hoppers for their dinner.

'Never mind,' he said. 'Dias-*mahathaya* has gone.'

I was surprised, but pretended not to be and shrugged.

'And for you, Sir?'

He shook his head. 'No food.'

'But Sir, have something,' I said.

He thought for a moment looking round the kitchen. He saw my small pagoda of wicker steamers on the side counter ready for the strings. A shadow seemed to pass over his face. 'Sandwich,' he eventually said. 'Just bring a sandwich.'

*

COOK'S JOY

DESPITE HIS apprehension, Mister Salgado took the job. Soon he was out of the house on a regular basis. He would roar out in his car at eight-thirty and return only at about quarter-to-one; I would feed him; he would disappear into his room for a nap and then, usually some time after two, set off back to the office. Some days he would go on tour, racing down to his observatory on the coast. He would be gone for days, right down past Joseph's home town to where the deep south bottoms out and begins to curve up again—the enchanted region of exorcists, devil-dancers and wild elephants from the days even before the good Lord Buddha appeared to free us from our demented demons. On these occasions, I would have plenty of time on my own: the world became boundless. There was a lot to do. I learned early on that nature takes her course unless you work hard: things go out of control. Rooms get silted up, doors lose their hinges, the kitchen grows black mould and you have to fight your way in darkness. But I found I could keep order in a few hours and still find time for a life of simple pleasure. Dr Balasingham, next door, had prudently emigrated with his family to an Appalachian cabin in America, and I lost my feather-headed companion, but it didn't matter. I had progressed in my reading. I spent a lot of time in my master's study poring over his *Reader's Digests* and *Life* magazines, his almanacs. He had a low table by the shelves and after his bath he would sit cross-legged on it with a book on his lap. I could feel the air move when he turned a page, each one catching the lemony light slice by papery slice. I too liked to sit unfettered in a room of my own, emptied of all the past, nothing inside, nothing around, nothing but a voice bundled in paper, a pattern of marks entering my own stillness. Feeling someone inscribing the soft grey tissue of my brain, writing on water, and rippling my mind. I would sink in, the skin of the book rubbing against the skin of my thumb and forefinger. Taking in thought after thought I would forget where one began and the other ended. The only sound the sound of onion-skin rustling from story to story like trees blowing in a summer orchard.

But I also hankered after the real world; I wanted to see Mister Salgado's famous ocean and the life beyond our garden gate. I got my chance the day Mr Dias fell into a sewage hole.

It happened just outside our house. A new bungalow was being built on the fifteen perches of wasteland next to number ten, and a pit had been dug extending out into the lane. There were thick planks of wood on each side. Dias, instead of walking in the middle of the road like any sensible person would, had headed for the edge. Suddenly the two Alsatians at number ten rushed to the gate snarling and Mr Dias jumped like a hare; two seconds later he slipped and fell into the pit. I had to go and help him out. He was covered in thick red mud and was swearing like I had never heard him before: 'Shit, shit, shit. Bloody damn-fool fucking shit.'

'What a shit-hole!' he said to Mister Salgado when he got inside the house. He looked so grumpy he was like somebody else. 'A real shit-pit!' he said to me.

Mister Salgado announced, 'I am taking Dias-*mahathaya* to the observatory, you also come.'

I asked him, 'Sir, what to take?'

'Just the normal things.'

But what did *normal* mean? There was nothing normal about living in that extraordinary house, heading for nothing but oblivion, as far as I could tell. 'But Sir, will I be cooking or what?' Usually when he went on his own I only packed his clothes: his khaki drill trousers, the yellow bush-shirt, swimming-trunks, his Jockey Y-fronts and white socks; hard, brown walking boots in a separate bag. On his own he would stay at a Rest House nearby. But if we were all going, I was not sure what the arrangements would be.

'Yes, you will have to do the cooking. Wijetunga has only a small *kolla* there. You'd better bring linen and things also. We'll all stay at the bungalow.'

I had to get condiments too, flour, oil—the basics—in a carton. Beer and water, tea, milk powder, sugar. An ice-box with bacon and butter. My frying-pan, my butcher's knife: there were so many things. I wanted to make sure everything would work perfectly wherever it was we were going.

When Dias reappeared after a shower and having changed his clothes, Mister Salgado got us together and fired questions: most of the things I had packed, but there were a few, like his Leica and his radio, which I had not thought of; they were for him to decide on, not me. I rushed around fetching stuff and nonsense from all over the place and piled it up under the porch: a small mountain of portable civilization mined out of the old house and ready for storing in the back of the Land-Rover.

Mister Salgado liked to do the actual arranging of the inside of the vehicle himself. He opened the back and started to put the boxes in. I helped him. 'No, put that over in the corner . . . Good. Now this one here.' It was masterly. He knew exactly what shapes fitted together to make the best use of space. My mountain of goods disap-peared into a geometry of storage that was smaller than a camp-bed, all planned in his head.

Dias clucked approvingly. '*Sha!* Excellent packing. How you got it all in, *men*! Real genius.'

'Right, Dias, are you ready?'

'Ready for anything. Let's see this bloody ocean of yours.'

Mister Salgado then looked at me. 'Everything locked up? Doors and all?'

I hurtled around the house like a bluebottle. The back door had to be bolted, but there was nothing more to do. When I got back to the porch I found the other two already in the vehicle. Mister Salgado in the driver's seat, as always, and Dias next to him in the front.

He eased the vehicle forward and out of the gate, which I shut and carefully locked with a galvanized slave-chain. 'Get in,' Mister Salgado said, pointing behind his shoulder with his thumb. I jumped into the back, and we were off.

'Ah, the warm South . . . ' Mister Salgado mumbled, shifting smoothly into top gear as we cruised down under the big shade-trees.

'What?'

'Poetry.'

'What poetry?'

'English poetry. My father used to recite poetry just like that.'

'Oy, oy, mind that bloody cow!'

Mister Salgado heaved on the wheel and we swerved to the right hitting the tail, but fortunately nothing else, of the passing animal. Dias started laughing, 'You hit it, you got it.' His head was bobbing up and down. Mister Salgado looked worried. Out of the back I saw a rickety body sway; the cow hobbled across the road, high on adrenalin but not seriously hurt. Mister Salgado's fingers were clenched over the wheel and he was staring straight ahead. He said nothing. Dias kept bouncing with laughter, blue smoke escaping from his mouth. He shook as he laughed, and his head continued to bob up and down on his round, fat shoulders. I was not very happy. It was not auspicious to smack a cow, the source of milk and labour. Even if you were thinking of poetry and going to save the island from the sea and the mind from forlorn darkness, it could not be right. Fortunately we soon came to a big temple by a bridge. Lorries and buses had jammed the road. We had to stop.

'Are you going to put your ten cents here, for the gods?' Dias asked.

Mister Salgado shrugged. People were praying by the *Bo*-tree inside the temple square, and drivers and travellers stuffed money into a blessing box in the wall. I leaned forward, 'Sir?' I thought we should.

'All right, you go. But be quick.'

I jumped out and put ten cents in the box for all our sakes and brought my hands together in a rush, almost in applause rather than worship. Ten cents perhaps balanced the business with the moony cow on the road.

'OK?' Mister Salgado asked when I climbed back in.

They were both indulging my unenlightened habits, they thought, but I was not a believer. In my own way I am a rationalist, same as Mister Salgado, but perhaps less of a gambler; I believe in tactical obeisance, that's all. If there is a possibility that the temple exerts some influence, that there is some force or creature or deity or whatever that is appeased by ten cents in a tin box, why take a chance? At worst the ten cents will help keep the place tidy, or fill the belly of a monk who otherwise would be making some mischief on the streets. So I dropped the coins in the box thinkingly, not unthinkingly as I am sure Mister Salgado and Mr Dias thought I did.

Looking at them from behind, I discovered a tremendous difference between them, especially between their ears. Of course they were both intelligent, educated men, but Dias's ears were small and firmly pinned to a skull from which a small puff of tobacco smoke would periodically be released. His ears were hardly distinguishable from the rest of the head, still forming: a foetus ear, a bud, insensitive to the calls of nature—my earlier calls for a piss-stop, 'Sir, *su-barai!*'—whereas Mister Salgado had such a clearly articulated pair. Each an elegantly cupped, long, slender hand attached by a flared stem to the side of the head, exactly midway between top and bottom, and shrouded by his black hair; the lobes divinely long. These two heads and their distinctive ears seemed, for a moment, to belong to two different species come together only because of the confines of a vehicle and the thread of a common tongue. I touched my own ears to try and visualize their trumpet shape. Mine were big—bigger than Dias's anyway—but I pulled the lobes to lengthen them some more. The longer the better, my uncle used to say and, after all, I was still growing. Dias, on the other hand, had done all his growing.

Dias was born during the time of the British. He was a toddler on Galle Face Green when the Japanese attacked Colombo in 1942. 'Six Zeros came and I ran like hell for cover,' he used to say as a party piece. For a long time after I first heard this story in our dining-room with the rice steaming and fingers drumming, I thought he was talking of money falling out of the sky like they used to say happened to people in England where everyone became rich after the rain. Six zeros, ten lakhs, a million rupees, and I thought maybe that was how Mister Salgado also ended up as well-off as he was. But later, I understood he was talking about aircraft. They zoomed in from nowhere beyond the edge of the sea carrying a load of bombs to blast the island—the first blasts of their kind. Explosives rather than sixteenth-century *parangiya* cannon-balls. Harbingers of the self-mortification to come forty years later with our squadrons of reconditioned MiGs and their drums of home-made napalm, imitating a war in heaven more terrible than any kamikaze pilot might have imagined. Dias, ears flattened, bumped into a gram-seller's cart on the pavement and toppled a basin full of peanuts to the ground. The din apparently so excited a colonel who was shouting filth at the sky that he shot himself in the foot. 'The rifle, you see,' Dias would say, slightly inebriated, 'was resting like a fancy brolly on the tip of his shoe. In all the excitement, what with the din and all, the fellow pulled the trigger. Blew his own bloody big toe off!' It was the only casualty on the green. He had to be rushed to the hospital. Baby Dias was given such a scolding that he crawled into his cot and slept for twelve hours, sucking his aluminium identity tag, while the rest of the city braced itself for invasion. A few more shots were fired, an aircraft came down in some paddy-field and the Japanese warplanes disappeared back into the fluffy red sun. The course of the war swerved and luckily forgot this spot where a few lucky Allied soldiers and sailors spent the rest of their time battling with pawpaws and prickly pears, happily gathering memories of a tropical idyll for their retirement bungalows in Eastbourne and

Chichester. Meanwhile little Mister Salgado, mesmerized by stories of gravity, peanuts and the gunshots manifested around his friend baby Dias that fateful April, became a prodigy of science and a lover of poetry: 'Motion,' he would say in a deep, intimate voice to cap his dear friend's story, 'the secret is in the motion.'

In my childhood, at school, I learned language and history, some geography and sums; but science was a big black hole. My eager schoolteacher abandoned science to nature, assuming we would absorb the essentials through inquisitive play. Language, he used to say, was what made us different from the apes, and that was what he wanted to teach. But from my Mister Salgado I learned the reverse: language is what you pick up naturally—everyone speaks, no problem—but science has to be learned methodically, by study, if one is ever to emerge out of the swamp of our psychotic superstitions. It is what transforms our lives. The electrification of the village or the illumination of the mind, which comes first? he would ask his friend Dias. How far do you get reading *ola*-leaf books by moonlight and going slowly blind? But Sir, I wanted to ask, how do you thread magnesium filaments and copper alloys and turn electric longings into attractive voltage without learning to read and write and tell the past from the present? How can you tell that the brightening of the bulb on the wire follows from you flicking a switch on the wall without a sense of history and narrative? Otherwise it may seem that somehow a divine light, emanating from an all-powerful bulb, had caused in its infinite wisdom your hand to stroke that beautiful baroque switch, rather than the other way round. My Mister Salgado had studied all these things. He had travelled all over the earth. That was probably why for him everything *was* motion: motion explained everything. But it was not obvious to me. To be fair he did also make the point, mischievously, that the science is only as good as the thinking behind it. Without a secure framework the science eventually falls apart: in ten years, a hundred years or a thousand. When Dias once asked him, 'So, *men*, what is this damn frame you need behind it?' Mister Salgado replied, 'The right philosophy. Either you choose to observe and classify, or you choose to imagine and classify. It is a real dilemma.'

'But is that all?'

'It is *everything*.'

We drove for hours; whistling over a ribbon of tarmac measuring the perpetual embrace of the shore and the sea, bounded by a fretwork of undulating coconut trees, pure unadorned forms framing the seascape into a kaleidoscope of bluish jewels. Above us a tracery of green and yellow leaves arrowed to a vanishing-point we could never reach. At times the road curved as though it were the edge of a wave itself rushing in and then retreating into the ocean. We skittered over these moving surfaces at a speed I had never experienced before. Through the back window I watched the road pour out from under us and settle into a silvery picture of serene timelessness. We overtook the occasional bus belching smoke or a lorry lisping with billowing hay; we blasted through bustling towns and torpid villages. We passed churches and temples, crosses and statues, grey shacks and lattice-work mansions. Mister Salgado only slowed down when we came to the skull-heaps of petrified coral—five-foot pyramids beside smoky kilns—marking the allotments of a line of impoverished limemakers, tomorrow's cement fodder, crumbling on the loveliest stretch of the coast. 'Look at that stuff,' he said to Dias. 'Goes by the ton.'

When we got to the bungalow—his observatory on the beach—I spent the rest of the day doing what I always did: putting things away, making the beds, getting the food ready, serving, clearing, cleaning, sorting, shutting up. But every time I looked out of the windows, it took my breath away. The bungalow itself was shrouded with huge green leaves luminous with sunlight, shading yet illuminating. The sand garden, the clumps of crotons, the vines around the trellises by the kitchen, all seemed to breathe with life. Inside, the rooms were small; the walls were painted a cool green and the floors had turned dark. Even the furniture seemed stained by the shade, but when I looked up again I would glimpse the sea between the trees bathed in a mulled gold light. The colour of it, the roar of it, was overwhelming. It was like living inside a conch: the endless pounding. Numinous. You couldn't get away from it. No wonder Mister Salgado said the sea would be the end of us all. During those two nights we spent on tour I felt the sea getting closer; each wave just a grain of sand closer to washing the life out of us. They say the sea air makes you feel better, but I reckon that must be to lull us to sleep; it made me feel helpless. After a while it terrified me. And it was no comfort when we eventually got to see Mister Salgado's instrument that was going to save us all from a watery grave. A black plastic binder filled with grids and numbers that his assistant, Wijetunga, recorded twice a day after measuring the tide-mark on the beach and counting the corals, sea-slugs, angel-fish, urchins, groupers and barracudas he happened to see as he snorkelled along a buoy-line stretched between two posts stuck in the sea. This seemed feeble in the face of the ocean's huge ripples, but I didn't say anything to Mister Salgado or Dias at the time. I asked Wijetunga, later in the evening after I had fried the fish, whether that was all there was to it. Numbers on a slate at the seaside. But having spent so much time underwater examining convoluted prehistoric life-forms, he seemed unable to speak. It looked as though his heart were full of desire—a need—for expression, but his mouth permanently corked; holding in his breath. He was an educated man, with neat, tiny handwriting. He wore black trousers when Mister Salgado asked him to join them at mealtimes. But he always looked uncomfortable, as if choking on his own thoughts. When I spoke to him, he rubbed his broad rubbery nose with the palm of his hand and sighed noisily, thinking, I suppose, of how impossible it was to deal with my ignorance. He mumbled through his hand something about timing and diving.

Dias was also, I think, not entirely convinced. After tucking into my fish-balls and a huge helping of red rice, he washed his fingers in a bowl of lime-water and said, 'I don't know, *men*, I am not much of a sea-bather, but I find this ocean is very big, no? Isn't it? I mean for us to really do anything?' Faced with this sea he was not keen even on a boat trip.

Mister Salgado drew in his breath. Whenever he felt threatened he drew breath. His chest would inflate and his hands would swell up. He crossed his arms. 'The ocean?'

Dias lit a cigarette and puffed vigorously, building up a good head of smoke. 'I mean this dipping a stick in here and there, how will it tell you what is happening when thousands of miles away, like in Australia, a whole bunch of whales may be humping or something. That'll make this millimetre here and there all cock-eyed, no?'

'Whales don't go in for orgies.'

'I know, I know. But you know, no, what I mean? A bit of hanky-panks.'

I could see the shape of Mister Salgado's tongue as it travelled around his mouth, running over his teeth just under the lips making the skin ripple. 'Wijetunga here is not measuring millimetres. He is examining samples. You can tell a helluva lot from a sample, if it is thoroughly observed. You know, as if I sliced just a tiny bit of skin from your finger, or took just one strand of your hair . . . ' He reached forward as if to pluck it.

'Oy! Thank you, thank you, but leave my hair out of this. Precious bloody few here as it is.' Dias patted his polished forehead.

'But really, just with one strand, or a bit of tissue, we can analyse it and tell you everything about your biological history.'

Dias laughed. 'Uh-huh-ha, yes, yes. That I can believe. Let me tell you I also, as an accountant—even a government accountant—can tell you a helluva lot: one helluva lot. If I know a man's salary and his age I can tell you his whole *biographical* history—his life story past, present and future, you know.' He pursed his lips.

Wijetunga looked flustered, but he said nothing. Mister Salgado chuckled, 'That's it. Same thing. Imagine the globe as a head. You see, you only need a tiny bit of information to build the whole picture. And the most important bit of information is in movement. The motion of a wave.' He relaxed now. 'The tiny vibration, the sound wave for example, that might take centuries to evaporate. If we had the instruments sensitive enough to measure it, that wave could tell us the conversation your great-grandmother might have had with your great-grand-father on their wedding night a hundred years ago.'

'You mean that naughty talk is still going round?' Dias twirled his finger in the air, sloshing the arrack in his glass and giggling. The sea was booming so loud I reckoned every wave, sound or otherwise, would be obliterated forever. 'So, you have this kind of instrument for the ocean?'

'It's an idea. We are working on it. But we have no fancy lab yet.'

'Bullshit, *machang*, bullshit.'

Mister Salgado laughed.

I was working on the curry rings on their dirty dinner-plates, scientifically applying a tuft of coconut hair and lime-water to the yellow grease. I was scrubbing my heart out. It was no joke.

*

BEFORE MISS Nili first came to our house on the *poya*-holiday of April 1969, Mister Salgado only said to me, 'A lady is coming to tea.' As if a lady came to tea every week. It had never happened before in his life, or mine, and yet he acted as if it were the most natural thing in the world. Luckily he gave me some warning. He was concerned to make sure there was plenty of time to prepare, even though he acted so nonchalant. I made everything: little coconut cakes—*kavum*—patties, egg sandwiches, ham sandwiches, cucumber sandwiches, even *love-cake* . . . I made enough for a horse. It was just as well: she ate like a horse. She finished all the patties! And her piece of love-cake—I left it to her to cut—was enormous. I don't know where she put it; she was so skinny then. So hungry-looking. I expected her to bulge out as she ate, like a snake swallowing a bird. But she just sat there on the cane chair, one leg coiled under her, her back straight and her face floating happily in the warm afternoon haze while huge chunks of the richest, juiciest love-cake disappeared into her as into a cavern.

'You like cake?' he asked her stupidly.

She made a lowing sound between bites. It made him happy, and although I didn't approve of her being quite so uninhibited so soon in our house, I was touched too.

'Where did you get this, this cake?' Her lips glistened with my butter, and one corner of her mouth had a line of golden semolina crumbs which smudged into a dimple as she spoke.

'Triton made it,' my Mister Salgado said. *Triton made it*. It was the one phrase he would say with my name again and again like a refrain through those months, giving me such happiness. *Triton made it*. Clear, pure and unstinting. His voice at those moments would be a channel cut from heaven to earth right through the petrified morass of all our lives, releasing a blessing like water springing from a river-head, from a god's head. It was bliss. My coming of age.

'Your cook?'

Your life, your everything, I wanted to sing pinned up on the rafters, heaven between my legs.

'He makes a lovely cake,' she said, endearing herself to me for the rest of my life.

I had used ten eggs instead of the regulation seven that day, because of her. And real yellow butter creamed to perfection. And *cadju*—cashew nuts—fresh from the countryside.

After tea she said she had to go. I went to get a taxi for her. She stayed with him alone in the house while I went up to the main road. It didn't take long. A black tortoise of a taxi with a butter-coloured top came along, and I rode in it like a prince back to the house. The driver croaked the old horn warning them of our approach. We rolled in right up to the porch. I got out and held the door open while Mister Salgado helped her in. 'Bye-bye,' she said to him and then turned to me. 'That cake was *really* good.'

The taxi rolled down to the gate and veered to the left. The wheels wobbled, making the whitewalls around the rim go fuzzy. Mister Salgado watched the vehicle slowly disappear.

'The lady ate well,' I said brightly.

'Yes.'

'Sir, the love-cake was good? *Really* good?'

'Yes.'

'I made it yesterday and gave the honey good time to

soak in. And the patties also she liked? Not too oily? I used fresh oil—brand-new bottle of Cook's Joy—especially for today.'

'They were good.' He turned to go back in.

They were more than good. I knew, because I can feel it inside me when I get it right. It's a kind of energy that revitalizes every cell in my body. Suddenly everything becomes possible and the whole world, that before seemed slowly to be coming apart at the seams, pulls together. I could squeeze a thousand string-hoppers through a wooden mould or embrace a whole hog when I feel like that. I had made mutton patties that day and put green coriander leaves in them; unheard of anywhere else in our country at that time. But however confident I was about the perfection of what I produced, like everybody else, I needed praise. I needed his praise and I needed her praise. I felt stupid to need it, but I did.

'Yes,' Mister Salgado sighed to himself and disappeared. His big, brown eyes brimming like the monsoon sea.

She came again the following *poya*-day—the lunar weekend as decreed by our leaders who thought the four phases of the moon should be used to eclipse the hegemony of the Judaeo-Christian imperial sabbath—and then regularly almost every weekend after that for months. I made mutton patties and a small cake every time, and she always said how *wonderful* they were. I did not bother with sandwiches or anything else after that first tea-party. Mister Salgado ate nothing: he watched her eat as if he were feeding an exotic bird. He drank tea. He always drank lots of tea: estate-fresh, up-country broken orange pekoe tip-top tea. He looked completely content when she was there. His face would be bright, his mouth slightly open with the tips of his teeth just showing. It was as if he couldn't believe his eyes, seeing Nili sitting there in front of him. I would bring the patties in four at a time on one of our small, blue willow-pattern plates, fried only after she arrived to ensure they came fresh and hot-hot, straight from the pan. The timing had to be perfect. I would offer her the patties and place the plate on the table. Always with a nice white lace doily. When she finished the last of the first batch, I would wait a minute or two before bringing in a second plate. 'Nice and hot-hot, Missy,' I would say, and she would murmur her approval. After she finished a couple of the new patties, I would come again with fresh tea. 'More patties?' She would shake her head—I would always ask when her mouth was full. This allowed Mister Salgado to speak on her behalf. 'No, bring the cake now.' It was our little ritual. I would nod, she would smile and he would look longingly. I would give her enough time to savour the aftertaste of the patties and feel the glow of coriander inside her. Let the tea slip down to cleanse her palate and subdue the nerves that had been excited by the spice and fattened by the meat, and only then bring out the cake on a small Dutch salver for Mister Salgado to cut.

She never finished the whole cake, although sometimes I think she could have without difficulty. But as Mister Salgado hardly ate more than a sliver, and that only after she had urged him again and again, there was always a good part left over. Mister Salgado lived off it for the rest of the week, a piece a day when he came back from his office in the late afternoon. Perhaps remembering her last visit as he slowly ate, the scent from her fingers, which might have brushed a crumb on the plate, mingling with the aroma of rose-water, almond essence, cardamom, letting her rise and settle in his imagination as the honey seeped into his body. I too sneaked a piece from time to time.

Later in the evening, after she had gone, he would emerge from his study and look out at Venus beckoning in the sky. As night fell we would retreat into the old world of ourselves. When he told Dias about Miss Nili, he made her seem to belong to something impossibly distant. 'You know, I can't really say . . . '

Dias twitched his shoulders in mock pain and clasped his hand to his heart.

To me, Mister Salgado said even less. He was completely preoccupied with her. Only her presence seemed to ease him. When she came she would talk between mouthfuls and stitch their weeks and months together into a seamless pattern. She would get him to talk too, more and more. 'Do you remember the first time we met?' she asked him one afternoon after I brought out the cake.

'At the Sea Hopper?'

'No, before. You remember?'

Mister Salgado said he remembered wanting her to turn towards him in the ballroom of the Sea Hopper Hotel, where she worked, when he had seen her there at some reception. Willing her to turn. And, miraculously, she had turned and looked at him, but he had not known what to do. 'I can't remember what I said. I wanted to say *sorry*, but I didn't want to remind you . . . '

'Of stepping on my toe?' She laughed, raising her foot and massaging it.

' *Your* first word was a yelp . . . '

78

'*Aiow!*' she mimicked. 'And your first touch was a hard, pointed shoe crunching my poor toes!' That had been their first encounter; outside a bookshop under the arches in the Fort. There had been nothing more to it, but it served as an introduction.

'I was checking some book I had bought. I didn't know what I was doing. If only I'd looked where I was going . . . but then we'd never have talked.'

She placed her hand on his. He smiled happily.

He seemed so radiant when she was there with him that I wished she would come more often and lift the monkishness from our monastic house.

*

ONE MORNING Miss Nili arrived in a taxi after Mister Salgado had gone to his office.

'Sir is not here,' I said. 'He has gone to the office.'

'I know. I want to talk to you.' She told the driver to wait and came up into the house. 'Triton, I want to see one of his shirts.'

'Missy?'

'I want one of his shirts. A good one. One that fits nicely, not like that yellow bush-shirt; something longer, bigger.'

I had tried to get rid of that yellow bush-shirt many times. It was an awful shirt, left over from his youth. Although it appeared to fit him from the front when he looked in the mirror, it had lost its shape and was ridiculously short when seen from any other angle. But Mister Salgado had never seen what it looked like from behind or even from the side; he would search it out and determinedly wear it. His blue shirt was much better, more manly, and I mentioned it to her. 'Or if you come, I can show all his wardrobe,' I said. She could choose for herself. I was sure that he would be pleased for anything of his to be in her hands.

She looked a little startled, but her eyes brightened. She followed me into the bedroom.

We crossed to where the almirah and chest of drawers stood. I led the way, listening to her leather slippers smacking my polished floor behind me. I opened the varnished doors. 'All the shirts are here.'

'What a nice room,' she said looking around. The big, brown bed faced the window which opened on to the side garden with its two temple-flower trees. She went up to the window.

'House sparrows nest just above,' I said, 'in the eaves.' They started twittering and spluttering outside. She touched the curtains I had put up recently. The previous lot had been there for years. I went with Mister Salgado to the big emporium to choose the new cloth. He had agreed to my recommendation straight away. He wanted the place to look good. I told Miss Nili that they were new.

'Very nice,' she said but she was not looking at them, nor was she looking at me.

I picked out the shirt I had told her about. 'This one?'

She came up to me and took it. She shook it out and held it up at arm's length, imagining him filling it. 'Come here, Triton,' she said and pressed it against me. I had to laugh. Mister Salgado was a tall, broad-shouldered man, although in those days very thin.

'Don't laugh,' she said. 'It will fit you.'

'Missy . . .'

She smiled and lowered the shirt. She stared at it for a minute. 'I'll take this.'

'But what to say if he wants it?'

This time she laughed. 'I'll bring it back. I only want to show it to the tailor, for size, you know.' She quickly folded it up in her hands. 'I want a new shirt made for him. For a Christmas present. A real man's shirt. But it is a secret, you mustn't tell him, OK?'

'Yes, Missy,' I promised faithfully.

'Right, I must go. I'll drop this back later.' I followed her outside to the taxi which was still waiting, empty.

The driver was on his haunches, smoking a *beedi*. 'Right, right!' I said. '*Nona* ready.' He took a last puff and chucked the *beedi* away to the side and sauntered over. 'Hey, take that with you,' I yelled. I had swept the drive that morning and I got really angry. He looked at me as if I were mad. I opened the door for Miss Nili. She told him to take her down past Slave Island to some itty-bitty *koreawa* road where her tailor worked. An opium den, I reckoned.

I liked Nili. She had no airs. She treated people— everyone, top and bottom—as real people. Not like other ladies—the *nonas*—who screeched *chi, chi, chi* at their servants. I was glad for my Mister Salgado, I was glad he had met her and I was glad she kept coming. She was younger than him, in her mid-twenties: halfway between him and me. I was getting used to seeing her in the house and felt those months were wonderful for their freshness. When he came home for lunch that day I did not tell him that she had come to the house. I thought he might notice something, a trace of her perfume maybe, but then he probably imagined her scent around him all the time and would not know the appearance from the reality. Short of leaving her slipper, or some item of her clothing, or her handbag itself, none of which she would ever have done, there could be no sign of her visit save an impression of her: a mark on the furniture, her fingerprints on the curtain, her shape moving through the air, the imprint of her words. Ultimately, the fact that it had actually happened, that she had come and spoken to me and left, was undeniable but almost impossible to confirm. Even so I didn't dare open my mouth in case her presence showed by its impression on me.

Fortunately we managed to get through our paces without a single word passing between us. He came home and disappeared into his room; stepped out only when he expected lunch to be on the table. Found, as usual, that it

was: boiled rice, liver curry, bitter gourd. Nothing unto-
ward. He sat down; I served. He ate. He drank his glass of
water and retired to his room. A little later I heard the car
start and he went back to the office.

Normally after he finished lunch I would clear the
table, then eat and wash up. Later, after he left, I would
spend the afternoon day-dreaming. That day I kept
imagining her losing the shirt, being robbed, or being
kidnapped with it by the pimps and thugs outside the
tailor's den, and my connivance being discovered. To
stop myself worrying I started on some meatballs, which
required real concentration as our old mincer was a big
cast-iron beast with a spindle that pulled in anything
and shredded it. You had to push the meat in hard
through a funnel while turning the handle, and if you
were not careful your fingers would be mangled. After
that, at about four-thirty in the afternoon, I went out
into the garden to weed the chrysanthemum bed. We
didn't have a gardener: there was no point. Having other
people to do these things was always more trouble than
it was worth. Mister Salgado would never take charge
and it would become very complicated. 'Don't worry,
Sir,' I had said, 'I can manage on my own.' It is not
worth getting someone else to do something when it
takes twice as long to explain it as to do it.

Miss Nili did not come back that afternoon.

When Mister Salgado returned it was already dark. He
had a big brown-paper parcel with him. I took it from his
hand and he said there was another box in the car. I got
that too, holding it by the double-crossed string.

'I thought we should have a Christmas tree this year,'
he said, looking at the ground as if somehow his words

would make a tree sprout out at his feet. 'You know what a Christmas tree is?' he asked me, still staring down.

I hooked the box on to the same hand that was holding the parcel and used my free hand to shut the car door. 'Yes, Sir,' I said. Number twelve down the road had a tree lit up with coloured bulbs every December in the front of the house.

'Like this one?' he nodded at the box. 'To put in the sitting-room?'

I shook my head.

It turned out to be a plastic tree. A thin artificial stem about five feet tall made out of brown plastic sticks that had to be fitted together and pinned with fake green fronds. The other parcel had golden strands of glitter and tiny electric lights. The lights were a miniature version of the party lights I had seen in the garden of number twelve. Small coloured bulbs set in crinkle-cut silver foil. A nice idea. Mister Salgado put the tree together and then stepped back to examine his handiwork. 'Good, now you do the rest,' he said and left me to it.

Later, after his bath, I heard him rummaging about the wardrobe. 'Where is that blue shirt of mine?'

'Sir?'

'That blue shirt. You know my blue shirt, where is it?'

My head was spinning. There was a hole in my throat. 'Blue colour?'

'Yes.' He turned and looked at me. 'What is wrong with you? I want to wear my blue shirt.'

'Needs repairing, Sir.' I had never lied to him before. At least not since the wicked old days of Joseph.

'Why? What happened to it?'

I rediscovered the wish-factor in religion and forgot the

ethics. 'Sir, the button went.'

'Fix it then. Sew a button quickly and bring it.'

'But needs washing also, Sir.' I prayed he would not ask to see it and massaged the old arrow-dent in my head.

'What am I going to wear then?'

I quickly pulled out his yellow bush-shirt. 'This one, Sir. Also very smart.'

He slipped it on and set about getting into the rest of his clothes.

The next day Nili came by with the blue shirt. I told her what had happened, that he had been looking for it.

'What for?' she asked. 'Where was he going so special?'

I did not know. Maybe it was something to do with Christmas. I showed her the Christmas tree.

'That's nice, a nice little tree. What about decorations?'

I pointed out the tinsel. The electric bulbs I had strung around it.

'What, no balls? No silver balls? He didn't get anything else?'

I shook my head. Looking at it in daylight I could see it was a little bare. I wished I had not shown it to her. I would have made it better, I was sure, learning slowly on my own. I would have worked out what else was needed.

'Tell him you need to put more things on to make it pretty.' She handed me the shirt. 'I hope you didn't think I'd run away with it,' she laughed.

I smiled. I wanted to laugh with her.

'You can get decorations from Bambalapitiya. Shall I bring a box?'

'No, Missy. Our Sir will bring. I am sure Sir will be bringing more things today.' And if he didn't, I would get the balls—silver balls, gold balls, coloured balls—I'd get all the balls going for her.

She smiled. 'Yes. I'm sure you are right. He is very careful like that. Now remember, don't tell him about the shirt.'

After she left I looked again at the Christmas tree. What was it for anyway? We had never had one before; we never celebrated festivals before. Even in the early days, with Lucy-*amma* and Joseph, the months passed without a mark in our house. I remember Lucy-*amma* sometimes went to temple and lit incense for *poya* as the moon masked and unmasked itself. But she was not very devout. Joseph was a toper, nothing else as far as I could tell. He disappeared from time to time, but only to dive into the nearest *kasippu* tavern and drink with his harbour touts and junkies.

I washed the shirt and hung it out to dry. It didn't take long; I was able to iron it and put it away before he came home. He probably would not ask for it again, but it was best to have it ready.

*

THAT DECEMBER I roasted a turkey for the first time in my life. I had never done anything like it before. It was a big bird but except for its size, I had no problem. Lots of basting and plenty of salt and butter worked wonders. The stuffing of raisins and liver, Taufik's *ganja* and our own *jamanaran* mandarins was enough to moisten a desert.

Mister Salgado himself helped me with the temperature and time factors. He sat with a pencil and a piece of paper. How heavy was the bird? What settings did the oven have? How long did I roast a chicken for? A duck? Pork? What size? What weight? He pursed his lips thoughtfully and consulted a cookery book. He gave me instructions like a professor and went into absurd detail: the angle of the bacon on top of the breast, the streakiness of its fat, the rind. Once I discovered the right setting for the knob, and the number of hours to let it go, I stopped listening. Dry heat baking—big deal: when it comes down to it either you know how to handle a bird or you don't.

My big problem was how to keep the creature from rotting for a day and a half. Mister Salgado had ordered it for Christmas Eve, and it was delivered in the morning. He didn't think of what to do next. The bird weighed sixteen pounds—one hundred rupees' worth, the bill was tied to its claw. The creature could just about be squeezed into the oven but it would not fit in the fridge unless the whole thing was cleared out, and that was impossible: we were fully loaded for the party. The only thing I could think of doing was to wash it down, dry it thoroughly with a towel and marinate it in soy sauce, cloves, garlic and liquor, wrapped up in an old cotton sheet. I did so the morning it arrived, but by afternoon I was worried. A turkey is not like wild duck or *batagoya* or jungle fowl. Wild meat is tough; it can take our putrefying heat. The rotting pre-digests it, gives it some *taste*, but these puffed-up monsters are like white bread: a couple of hours and they begin to go bad. Mister Salgado sniffed at it and suggested ice. I bought two huge blocks and packed a tub with ice and turkey. Covered it with a brown gunny sack to keep the cool in.

Nili and six others, including some foreigners, were coming to our once and only Christmas party: a real dinner party. It was to be my big challenge. Nili had only come for snacks before; this was going to be a Christmas meal that had to meet a standard she, as a Christian, knew but which I had no idea of. Most of the preparation I did the night before, cooped up in the kitchen with the shrouded turkey. It was not too complicated. Only five dishes for the main course: turkey, potatoes, two green vegetables and the ham, then a ready-made Christmas pudding. A doddle compared with some of the meals I had had to do just for Mister Salgado and Dias on their own, when suddenly they would want this and that delectation as every mouthful detonated a memory in each of them sitting there eating and drinking and burping to kingdom come. With a little preparation and planning any emergency could be handled. Anything was possible.

The day of the party our Mister Salgado was maddeningly anxious. He kept coming into the kitchen to ask how I was doing. I didn't say much; there was no time to fool about explaining. I would just nod or say, 'Right. Everything fine,' and get on with the next job. He would watch me from the door until he felt reassured and then go back into the house until the nerve juice rose to the surface again and brought him back. 'OK,' I kept saying. 'Everything fine.'

'Turkey getting brown? Is it?' He looked around the kitchen, confused even as to where the oven was.

'Not yet, not yet. It will brown. Don't worry, Sir, I will get it nice and brown in the last hour.'

'Potatoes? What about the potatoes? You haven't forgotten the potatoes, have you?' His voice quavered. He had spotted them in a basin of water.

'Sir, potatoes go later.'

He reached for one, not convinced.

'Sir, I will get the clothes ready.'

He threw up his hands. 'No, no. I can do that. You concentrate on this. This turkey business everyone says is very tricky. Mustn't be too dry otherwise it will be like stale bread.'

'I know, Sir, I know. Mustn't be uncooked or it will be too bloody. But don't worry, everything will be fine.'

'She says even her mother never got it right.'

So? My heart opened inside me and spread a warm glow through my blood. My turkey was going to be the best she had ever had.

I set the table in the dining-room for the eight of them and decorated it with temple flowers and some left-over Christmas tinsel. The mats for the centre of the table I arranged into the shape of a cross. After a final tidy up I still had time for a wash and change before the guests were due to arrive. I wore my white sarong for the occasion.

Mister Salgado was also ready early. He sat in the front bay rubbing his feet together, while I broke extra ice in the kitchen. The big blocks from the day before had lasted well. They had become smaller, more like rocks or half-bricks than the freeze-blocks they originally came as, but still good ice. Sawdust and wood chips streamed away in a flood as they broke into pieces under the blunt edge of my meat cleaver.

Nili arrived with Professor Dunstable from England and his friend Dr Perera. They drove up in a cream-coloured car which they parked in the drive.

'Good evening!' I heard Mister Salgado greet them.

Nili was laughing. She had an infectious laugh. It started at her lips and seemed to slither down her throat with a sucking sound. You couldn't ignore it. Dr Perera started laughing too. Mister Salgado served the drinks himself. He wore his beige trousers which he had ironed to a knife-edge. He looked very smart. Nili came up to him and put her arms around his neck. 'Merry Christmas!'

' . . . and a Happy New Year!' he said and kissed her.

I went back to the kitchen to clean the potatoes. There was a good hour and a half to go before people would be ready to eat, but with only two burners on the stove I had to time everything like a stationmaster. Mister Salgado had decided dinner should be served at nine o'clock. Punctually. None of this lotus-eating business, he had warned.

I wanted to go and listen to more of the conversation; we had not had many new visitors like these before that Christmas. It was always only Dias or one or two of Mister Salgado's other friends, and their conversation tended to be much the same, week in and week out: cars, politics, gambling. Nili of course was different, but coming as she did only for tea there was not much opportunity for me to hear real talk. She and Mister Salgado tended to stare at each other a lot. Christmas dinner promised to change all that. It was the beginning of something new, even though I could never have imagined how our lives were to be transformed over the next year.

Miss Nili called out for me, 'Triton!'

I went to her as fast as I could.

'Triton, please can you bring me some lime juice?'

'And those nuts, bring those nuts,' Mister Salgado reminded me as I passed by.

I came back with a tray and served everyone. The others had also arrived. I did not know them either: Mohan Wickremesinghe, a recently qualified dentist, and his wife Kushi; a short but muscular American called Robert and another foreigner, Melanie, whose face was a sea of freckles fringed by startlingly orange hair. She was chatting with a familiar figure—Dias. From his head small smoke-rings puffed towards the ceiling. Mister Salgado had not said anything about Dias! I had not expected him; I should have. Mr Dias was one who would always turn up. The only surprise was that he had not been to one of our crazy tea-parties for Miss Nili already. I went back to the kitchen, counting, going over the guests in my mind, slotting them into place. Yes, there were eight guests, not seven, plus Mister Salgado. But my table was set only for eight. Another place would completely upset the symmetry.

'What has happened?' Mister Salgado had come to check the food again.

'Sir, Dias-*mahathaya* is staying for dinner? Christmas dinner?'

'Of course. He must have some of this turkey. Why? Did he say . . . '

I explained that I had been told there were only seven coming, not eight.

'So, six, seven, eight, what does it matter? The main thing is, have you put the potatoes to roast?'

I nodded.

'Will the turkey be nice and warm?'

'No problem about food, Sir . . . ' I had kept it cool for a whole day and night, what is the difficulty in keeping it warm for two indolent, tropical hours? But where to squeeze the extra place in, that was a problem.

It had to be on the left. From that side the extra person could see the Christmas tree while eating. More the merrier. I quickly did the rearrangement while the hubbub was high outside, thanking my lucky stars for noticing Dias. It would have been too embarrassing if when the guests were called to the table and took their places one was left standing like at a game of musical chairs. But for that slight miscalculation the rest of the plan was going well. Everything was bubbling nicely in the kitchen, the beer was flowing, the cashew nuts and the *del* chips crunching. I could hear the whoosh of soda, the murmur of pleasant conversation and above it all Mister Salgado, a little tight already, holding forth on the thermodynamics of the ocean in the Age of Aquarius, and the story of an ark a hundred thousand years ago made of words and floating on a sea of sound.

I took a moment to listen; I felt I could afford to. At times of intense pressure I sometimes suddenly feel there is nothing more I can do; everything will take its own course, I can let go. I stay still and become blissfully calm for a moment, and my moment stretches endlessly. I felt as happy as Mister Salgado in his grand moment of pleasure, a foretaste of the months to come when he would enjoy a life of true romance, social intercourse and effervescent parties. It would become the most gregarious period of his life. I was happy for him, even though the politics of the day ruled against such emotions: his new world was one that had no place in the future, as ordinary people saw it then. It was a bubbly world of gaiety that seemed to belong to a previous, more frivolous, generation. At the *kadé* on the main road the talk was on the need for revolution, or for a return to traditional values. Schemes abounded to deal with people's new expectations. But in our house none of that mattered. Mister Salgado blossomed. His face lightened and opened, and he filled out to become tangible for the first time in our little world. I was proud of him, as I expect Miss Nili was too with all their foreign friends there. I marvelled at how entertaining he could be: I had not suspected it of him despite his occasional bouts of sudden enthusiasm, usually after a drink or two with Dias, about the ocean and its hunger for land. Now, with Nili, he had become a real performer, expertly massaging his audience like a politician.

'You see,' he drew a circle in the air above them, 'think of ether, like the ocean, as a big invisible pond. And every sound made like a stone plopped into it. You see the ripples? History is written just like that. As for this terrific rain they tell us about—imagine twenty inches in a night—it can only be monsoon. Where else would you wake up in the morning and find the whole downstairs of your house under water, your bed floating? Day and night for forty days—helluva bad monsoon. So, for the fellow on his *padura*—his mat—watching the heavens come down and the flood rising, obliterating everything he knew, it must have been like the end of the world. But our *baas-unnaha*—our carpenter with his boat—would have been OK. For him, land turning into sea was no problem. It would have been welcome even. Only thing is, every creature that could move would have crawled into the boat: like those snails you see escaping from a really gushing drain.'

'So, this Noah was a carpenter in Negombo then?' the dentist—Mohan—asked. Everybody laughed.

'Why not? If this place was paradise . . . ' Mister Salgado opened out his hand.

'Yes, Adam's Peak. Have you ever climbed to the top?' Professor Dunstable craned his recently reddened neck.

'And were you not once part of Africa? The cradle of us all?' the woman Melanie added, creasing swathes of freckles around a pale varnished mouth.

'You could say Africa, the whole of the rest of the world, was part of us. It was all once one place: Gondwanaland. The great land-mass in the age of innocence. But then the earth was corrupted and the sea flooded in. The land was divided. Bits broke and drifted away and we were left with this spoiled paradise of *yakkhas*—demons—and the history of mankind spoken on stone. That is why we in this country, despite the monsoon, love water. It is a symbol of regeneration reflecting the time when all evil, all the dissonance of birth, was swept away in divine rain leaving the gods to spawn a new world. That was the real flood; Noah's is just an echo. The kings who built the great tanks maybe were remembering that cleansing flood, just as we do.'

'The tanks?'

'You know our tanks? The great reservoirs? Inland seas, really. That is why we say *muhuda*. These were engineering feats done in two hundred BC, in the golden age of the cities of Anuradhapura and then Polonnaruwa. Some were done even earlier. Huge areas were put under water through a hydraulic system that required our *yakkha* engineers to measure a half-inch change of water-level in a two-mile stretch of water. Imagine that! Real precision. Enough to match the Egyptian pyramid makers, you know. All for water: the source of our life, and death. Take malaria . . . '

I was spellbound. I could see the whole of our world come to life when he spoke: the great tanks, the sea, the forests, the stars. The past resurrected in a pageant of long-haired princes clutching ebony rods; red-tailed mermaids; elephants adorned with tasselled canopies and silver bells raising their sheathed, gilded, curved tusks and circling the bronze painted cities of ancient warlords. His words conjured up adventurers from India north and south, the Portuguese, the Dutch and the British, each with their flotillas of disturbed hope and manic wanderlust. They had come full of the promise of cinnamon, pepper, clove, and found a refuge in this jungle of demons and vast quiet waters.

'So what *men*, Ranjan, you are trying to make out this place is the first Jerusalem? What about Buddha's special haven and all that?'

'Ah yes, but remember this was also known as the Garden of Eden. It panders to anyone's chauvinism, you know: Sinhala, Tamil, aboriginal. Choose a religion, pick your fantasy. History is flexible.' Mister Salgado laughed and peered into the dining-room. 'Here,' he called out for me. 'More pineapple juice for the lady. And get the food now, OK?'

Robert was still thinking about Mister Salgado's earlier comment. 'Actually, you are right. Everyone here is always bathing, always in the river or at a pipe or a well. Splish-splashing. Those women with wet skin-clingers. A real fetish.' He looked at Miss Nili as if for confirmation.

I went and brought the juice as fast as I could, but by the time I got back the conversation had moved on to a report in the newspaper about the encroaching sea. The roaring sea.

When the food was ready I put everything on the table except the turkey. I didn't know whether Mister Salgado wanted to carve it, as he usually did with roast chicken, or whether on this occasion I should cut it to pieces myself. He was listening to the professor, swaying tipsily. Nili saw me and interrupted the conversation. 'I think Triton wants to ask you something.'

'Sir, how to serve the turkey? Shall I cut or what?'

We went into the kitchen and I opened the oven: the bird looked ready to burst, beautifully brown. Mister Salgado was pleased and looked immensely relieved. 'Ah, looks good,' he said happily. He closed his eyes for a moment.

'Sir, maybe people should see it first before cutting,' I suggested.

'I will carve it; it has to be sliced. Yes, put it on the table and I will carve it. Where's the knife? Serve the other things while I do that. You are sure it is cooked inside?'

'Yes, Sir.' It was done perfectly. 'Ready. Look.' I heaved it out and placed it on our biggest plate, the breast proud-ly puffed out.

'Oh, good, good,' he said beaming. 'Bring it, bring it.'

My muscles must have doubled that Christmas ferrying

the turkey in and out of the oven and from pan to dish, table to table, basting, tasting, hoisting.

By the time I got it to the dining-room Mister Salgado had shepherded his guests in. They were lining themselves up, and Nili was getting someone to change places so that the women were not all on the same side. I made my entrance with the turkey obscuring most of me; there were cries of pleasure and surprise: 'My God! Look at that bird!' and 'I say, *machang*!' and helpless murmurs of approval, the sucking of teeth, a familiar anticipatory burp from Dias. I placed the bird in front of Mister Salgado.

'Sit, sit,' he said to everyone.

'Carve, carve,' Dias urged.

I stood back for a moment and let the crowd settle. They made a lot of fuss about it, but it sounded a happy, excited fuss. I could see the meal was going to be a success even before anyone had taken a single mouthful: the mood was right, and mood, I am convinced, is the most essential ingredient for any taste to develop. Taste is not a product of the mouth; it lies entirely in the mind. I prepare each dish to reach the mind through every possible channel. The mouth I only need to tickle, get to salivate, and that I can do even by the picture I present, the smell—perfume rubbed on to the skin, or even the plate, uncooked—the sizzle of a hot dish or some aromatic tenderizing herb. For the mouth itself salt, sugar, lime and chilli alone provide a stunningly varied palette. And this evening this exotic bird needed very little from me to get the seated, already heady, imaginations to explode with sensation.

Mister Salgado kept his head down, concentrating. He produced three elegant slices from each side of the breast and, lifting the pieces with the broad blade of the knife, placed them on a plate. Steam rose from the white flesh. He looked around. 'Any takers for a leg? Melanie?'

'A slice of white for me please. I turned vegetarian last year. I thought you would all be out here. But this travelling—especially India—made me so weak I gave up.' Her mottled milky shoulders trembled as she forked her hair with her fingers.

Robert chuckled. 'Your blind Celtic munchies, you mean.'

'How divinely primitive. So, who? Dias?' Mister Salgado asked.

I saw Dias wanted a whole leg. His lips were moist. He tucked them in and glanced around the table.

'Go on . . .'

'All right, give me then, yes.'

'The whole leg?'

'No, no. Are you mad? Just cut some slices, *men*. Who can have such a huge leg?'

I served the vegetables. Then a ruby-red Jaffna wine Miss Nili had winkled out of a dry-zone vicar, especially for Mister Salgado. She told the others that it came from one of the finest collections in the country. The vicar hand-painted the labels on the bottles himself. Everybody watched her while she talked, and Robert especially seemed to take in every word. Between episodes she urged me to serve more as though she were the hostess instead of the chief guest. I was happy to oblige and watch while I waited.

The nape of her neck was bare. Her dress hung suspended by two thin black straps. She had pinned her hair up at the back with a silver clasp. Some of the hair had slipped out, but I could still see a swollen red lump like a mole, or a bite, on the left side of her neck along a downy tendon. It slid as her skin stretched when she moved her head in response to someone talking. Her ears moved too when she spoke. They were larger than I expected. Each with two symmetrical wrinkles where they joined her neck and the outer edges curled in like the edge of a puppadum when it hits hot oil. My instinct was to press the ears back with my hands and keep the entrances to her soul open like the lips of a glazed pink conch. Perfume rose up from her, and when I moved in to spoon the potatoes on to her plate it seemed the scent was stronger. It rose up from below her throat down inside her flapping dress. She had her elbows on the table; her body was concave. She must have smeared the perfume with her fingers, rubbing it in like honey paste to enrich the skin. She finished her story and lifted her hand to stop me ladling more on to her plate. My sarong, tight around my hips, brushed her arm. She didn't notice. She was looking across the table. Robert had caught her eye; he was smiling, his head shyly cocked to one side. A piece of turkey tumbled from her fork. She quickly retrieved it and said, 'Jesus!'

'Jesus!' the others all murmured lifting their fermented raisin juice.

'The Age of Aquarius!' Nili added sparklingly.

Robert laughed and clapped his hands.

I whipped around to the other side and served Dias. 'Potatoes, Sir?'

He winked at me.

I piled them on.

'Triton, you made this Savoy-style, no?'

I nodded, embarrassed, as if I had been caught playing on the wrong side of the road. 'Our Sir wanted something special,' I said softly so that only he would hear.

He leaned towards me. 'But you have some *katta sambol* or something? Green chilli? Bring some. *Poddak* huh? Just for the taste only.'

Mr Dias was an addict. He could taste nothing in his mouth except chilli. He needed it like other people needed coffee, to wake the nerves inside him. Maybe it was because he smoked so much. Everything inside was wreathed in smoke. If I had known he was coming I would have doubled the spice in the sauce, enough to cut through to him instead of having to smuggle it in. If the others saw it, the chilli would spread everywhere and my turkey sauce would be completely spoiled. 'I'll bring it in a minute,' I said and moved on.

Mister Salgado had finished carving; he beckoned me. Without speaking he indicated that I should put the carcass on the table, in the middle.

'Where, Ranjan, did you get your turkey from? With these import restrictions changing all the time, I couldn't find *anything*.' Kushi-*nona*, the dentist's wife, dug the raisins out of the stuffing and examined them closely.

Mister Salgado explained he had got it from Peacock House. 'Some chap started a turkey farm near Alawwa and he supplies Peacock House with the birds. This is his first season, I think.'

Dias giggled. 'I bet the fellow has a peacock on his turkey farm, no?'

'Di-as!' Nili poked him in the ribs. 'Don't be so silly.' She laughed, throwing her head back. I could see the meat slide down her throat.

'I have met him,' Dr Perera said. 'Fernando, Maxwell Fernando. Enterprising chap. I don't know how he got his turkeys, but he has discovered some scheme by which he can get the fellows pumped up very economically. He made a damn good deal on that.'

'In that case, I hope *you* didn't get caught out?' Melanie touched Mister Salgado's arm comfortingly.

'Only one turkey, and just once a year. What is the harm in letting this Fernando prosper a little? We have to support these fledgling entrepreneurs.' He shrugged. 'They are the only *artistes* we have, you know, of our times . . .'

I finished serving and retreated to the doorway. Knives and forks clattered, chopping and scooping. Professor Dunstable's mouth was working furiously: it seemed to tighten into a tiny flower when he chewed his food. Each mouthful was pulverized and squeezed around and around until it pushed out his lips as if it were about to be spat out, but then he would swallow and the ball of mush would shoot down his gullet. Mohan Wickremesinghe watched him with professional interest.

I could not see Miss Nili's face but I could see her arms moving, cutting and tucking. Only Mister Salgado didn't eat solidly. He did not let me put very much on his plate. But he looked happy, gazing across at Miss Nili. Robert was nodding at Dr Perera, who was waxing lyrical about expeditions to the moon. Dias was carrying on a big conversation with Melanie and seemed to have forgotten his chilli. He was eating up everything on his plate. I reckoned for once maybe he would not miss the chilli.

In my father's village there used to be alms-days. I felt this was the same sort of thing. Only here it was to do with Jesus, although no one mentioned him again after the first toast. Mister Salgado at the head of the table looked as though he might be thinking along the same lines. It was not charity, but it was an act of giving. In my case, the giving was in transforming the intention into something edible. I gave by cooking and it gave me pleasure in return.

Masses of flesh were left on the turkey, and I thought I should carve some more and serve the rest of it. Mister Salgado nodded, approving.

Everyone had another helping; everyone except Mister Salgado. He liked to eat when he could relax alone in a loose sarong without having to engage in the talk around him. He preferred to concentrate on one thing at a time.

One by one the others reached their capacities and laid down their cutlery. When I came to take their plates there were little grunts of satisfaction, and a long, low burp from Dias. Robert looked me straight in the eye, his own irises packed with splintered bluish ice, and said a cool, neat thank you.

For dessert I offered the bought-in Christmas pudding, but I was not worried about that. Provided the guests had been well fed on the main course, I knew you could coast with the pudding.

Mister Salgado suggested coffee in the sitting-room, and people rolled off to their foam-cushioned roosts. I left the cups and saucers and a big pot of coffee for them to sort out however they wanted. Miss Nili poured while I cleared the dining-room with what I imagined was the professional clatter of the Sea Hopper Hotel. The foreigners left early with polite 'Merry Christmases' and 'Cheerios'. The others got on to a discussion about the recent release of the Major-General's cabal.

'Big mistake,' Mohan said. 'They are not just a bunch of army-navy puffers. It's not like in '62 when the only treason anyone could imagine was that half-baked cocktail coup.'

'Ah yes, and what about *Doctor* Tissa, this mysterious *Doctor* Tissa?' Dias wagged his finger in the air. 'I bet we hear more from him!'

'*Doctor* Tissa? Yes, who has so cleverly diagnosed discontent. But any bloody fool can tell you the youth are very discontented today. This bugger just wants to make trouble.'

'Who is he?' Mister Salgado asked.

'Some fellow they sent to Moscow on a scholarship. Now the joker wants to be a People's Hero. A revolutionary.'

I heard Miss Nili say that every day people came to the hotel where she worked, looking for jobs. They came with yards of qualifications.

'Trouble, trouble,' Mohan muttered and got to his feet. 'They want blood, not jobs. They want a purge. They want to destroy all of us.' He looked at his wife's dazzling teeth. 'Come, anyway let's go.'

'How about you, Nili? You want a lift? Or will Dias give one?'

'I will, I will.'

Later, after clearing up, I went to ask if anyone wanted more coffee.

'No, no. No more coffee,' Dias shook his head gravely. Then added, 'Very good, Triton. Excellent meal.' He turned to the other two. 'Fantastic cook, this fellow. First class. A real chef, no?'

Miss Nili said, 'Wonderful.'

I backed away.

'You go and have some now,' Mister Salgado said. 'Have that turkey.'

'Sir, what about for Sir?'

'Tomorrow. It'll be better tomorrow.'

'What? How can you say tomorrow . . . ' Nili was furious. 'What a stupid thing to say.'

Mister Salgado turned to me. 'It was good. Very good. I'll have some later on.'

I wished he would eat straight away. It was always awkward for me to eat his food before him. Sometimes when he didn't eat, I also had not to eat until the next day. Or find something else for myself. Otherwise he would be eating my leftovers. It was not right.

Back in the kitchen the table seemed to sag. It tired me just to look at the pile of plates and dishes and the half-eaten carcass; two hours of work there at least and it couldn't be left for the morning. If it were, the place would be swarming with rats and roaches. The turkey was still too big for the fridge with its breastbone sticking up like the rib of a tent. It had to be boned and then the dishes cleaned.

Boning in itself is a kind of rest: soothing. An after-hours affair. One can lose all sense of one's surroundings and become as one with the knife teasing out little scraps of flesh from cartilage and soft bone. The whole point of being alive becomes simplified: consciousness concentrated into doing this one thing. It is different from washing-up where there are so many different tasks. You have to think then, make decisions, discriminate: what to throw away, what to soak, what to clean. Only drying has anything like the simplicity and ritualistic beauty that boning has, but even that is spoiled by the need eventually to think about putting away what you have done. Boning is baser; like an animal devouring its prey, like eating but without consuming. A return to primal values. The thrifty hunter, a digestive process. A survivor, that's me. A sea-slug.

When I had cut off the parson's nose and worked my way about two-thirds up the backbone, Miss Nili came in.

'Triton, Happy Christmas!' she said quietly from the doorway.

I turned, half-hunched over my operating-table, not wanting to lose my place in the joint.

'I have a little present for you.'

I didn't know what to say; I said nothing.

'You know at Christmas-time we give presents, so I have a little something for you.'

But I had nothing for her. 'A present?'

She held out a small parcel.

I wiped my hands on a dishcloth but they still felt greasy. I couldn't touch it. 'Wait,' I said and quickly washed my hands at the sink again, rubbing with a scrub of coconut hair and pink whalebone. I wiped my hands on my sarong and took the parcel: a small rectangle wrapped in brown paper and decorated with green triangular shapes.

'*Aney* Missy, I haven't anything in return . . . '

'Don't be silly, Triton. Mister Salgado said you would like this.'

I could feel it was a book. I felt wretched and confused, and my throat was dry.

'Open it.'

I did not want to open it. The parcel seemed so beautifully wrapped. The corners neatly folded in and pasted. I had never received anything like it before. I had never been given a present in my life. 'A book?'

'Open and see,' she smiled.

I took my black-handled onion-cutter and slipped it in under the broadside flap and slid it gently along the pasted paper, releasing one surface from the other. Rice paste and the smell of pristine printed paper rose like smoke. I slipped the book out of the paper case, preserving the shape of the wrapping to house it again later. *One Hundred Recipes from Around the World*, illustrated, bound in hard cloth covers with a jacket showing dishes shooting out of a globe.

'It's a present,' she said. 'I hope you will like it.'

Like it? I could not believe that the thought might ever have crossed her mind. Why should she be concerned about me in that way? But having heard the words come out of her mouth I was amazed she could think that there might be some uncertainty about my response. As if I could ever not like it? As if I might *not* like the perfume of cinnamon in pearly rice, or the hum of a hummingbird sucking nectar from a pink shoe-flower?

She stood looking straight at me. I looked back briefly, for a couple of seconds at most, and realized I had never done it before. I glimpsed a startled bird-like face, her natural expression. I could not look back at her again, even though she had not flinched when our eyes met. She stayed motionless it seemed, while I gripped the book with both hands.

'It's been a good year, Triton. I hope it's been a good one for you too.'

'Yes, Missy.'

'I wish this year could go on forever . . . ' It was late. She was tired. She didn't know what she was talking about. I think she might have had more gin than lime in her fruit juice.

'Missy, next year will be good too. Maybe better.'

'I hope so, Triton,' she said. 'God, I hope it will be as good.' She looked around the kitchen, and I became conscious of the stacks of dirty plates and dishes. One counter was still piled up with stuff I had used for cooking. Despite my careful planning I had got too involved inside the house and had cut a few corners in the final stages to get the food on the table in time, all warm. There was a lot of work to do. The floor was a mess. It needed sweeping. Really it needed washing: a proper clean. But before I did that I would have to finish washing the dishes; put all the bits of potato and marrow and bone and turkey skin that people left on their plates—enough to feed a whole family on—into the bin, rinse and scrub with scouring powder and rinse again, so the floor would not get scrapped on and dripped on straight away; and before that there was the boning to finish and the parcelling and storing of the leftovers so that all the dishes for clearing and washing were primed and ready for cleaning. And my momentum in teasing the last of the turkey flesh from its bone had gone; the energy drained away as I stood speechlessly in front of her waiting for her lips to move. Eventually she said, 'That was a wonderful meal, Triton. Well done.'

I told her it was a new thing for me. I was not sure how good it really was. Whether it was better than her mother's.

'Wonderful, Triton. Have you had some?'

I shook my head. Where was the time?

'You have some. Have some now.' Despite her work at the hotel business she didn't know much about what one has to do to keep things in order. I could not eat now, there was too much to do. Hunger I can suppress. When it is just yourself you can put things off, you can do away with things; when you have to serve only yourself sometimes you let yourself off: there are no obligations. Eventually the stomach contracts to fit its circumstances as it so readily expands when times are good. 'Your Mister Salgado also never seems to eat,' she added. 'What is it about this house that makes it so hard for you men to eat?'

I smiled but said nothing. It had nothing to do with the house. It was the way we lived. Even though I wished he would eat with the others and give me a chance, I knew exactly how he felt. He needed his privacy to feel comfortable. When there were other things to attend to—people to talk to, guests to look after, ideas to pursue—eating would be too much of a distraction. There was no security in eating in the company of a lot of people; attention always got divided. Only the intimate could eat together and be happy. It was like making love. It revealed too much. Food was the ultimate seducer. But I could not tell that to Miss Nili. I had not even thought it through at the time. I was a virgin. In the end I said I would eat after I finished my work. Always eat at the end, then you can eat copiously, deservedly.

Even in the poor light of our kitchen, especially where she was standing, where the night seemed to seep in and darken the room even more, I could see the lines around her mouth deepen and the tip of her tongue—a piece of red, warm, inner flesh—move between her lips. Her teeth caught a bit of light from somewhere and tipped it into the kitchen. She was smaller than me, but standing there in the dark, talking, she seemed to grow in size. I felt her hand touch mine.

Inside the book there was a hundred-rupee note. A

piece of paper with drawings etched somewhere in Surrey: a picture, names that meant nothing to me; swirls of coloured ink. Valued simply by being possessed and not for anything intrinsic. Not for craftsmanship, not for the skill of someone who had given his whole life to become expert in the making of such designs, not for the few words carried, but simply for being recognized. It lay on the title page of the book.

'What is this?' I asked, but she had gone. *Missy*, I wanted to call out and bridge the gulf between us. I was only a servant, but I wanted there to be more than money between us in our small world. She would be talking with Mister Salgado and Dias already. I wondered whether they were all three exchanging presents too. I returned to the bird, smoothing the bone, greasing the skeleton. There was little else to me too: my flesh was melting, leaving me numb and empty. I felt stupid for not having made more of the time she was with me in the kitchen, for not finding out more. There was so much we could have talked about, but instead I was left with a silence punctuated only by the scraping of my knife, the rats scratching at the wall and the hordes of cockroaches feeling their way in our damp, dark cupboards. Her perfume had filled the whole place at first, overpowering the giddy smell of turkey; but now it seemed only to have left a trace of sourness in me.

When, with a twist of the liver-wing, I finally finished my task, I put the bones in a bowl to make a stock and packed the meat in a plastic container. That at last was something that fitted in the fridge humming on the veranda between the kitchen and the dining-room. A stray cat purred by it. I hissed at it and put the turkey in the coldest corner.

Inside the house I could hear Dias talking. He had had plenty to drink and was on good form. 'Fantastic!' I heard him say. His voice rose half an octave higher, 'Nili, you are fantastic.' She burst out laughing. Both their voices mingled with Mister Salgado's and poured out of the doorway into the back garden. In the dark the voices had a life of their own; they moved around me as if I were deep underwater and they were fish swimming, leaving a trail that could be felt but not seen, small currents, waves. There was a kind of insane quality about the laughter, and a deep reassuring undertow to the sound—I couldn't make out the words—of Mister Salgado. It mingled with the sounds of the rest of the neighbourhood. I imagined all of those who might be lying down in the houses of our street. At least two or three people in each house lying on their own, much as I would, on a mat in a corner of a room. There might be sixty such bodies lolling alone, prone, feeling only themselves, in our lane: a tide of blood swelling their flesh. Maybe another thirty couples, husbands and wives, lovers behind closed doors and open windows locked in some sweaty contorted embrace of love or affection or ritual. Thrusting and rocking the lane, house by house, in a unison they were blissfully unaware of; deliriously murmuring, or thinking about dinner or breakfast—or even their cook—while they made a kind of love to last the night. How many might have found someone new this night? What do they say to each other at times like this, in the dark, with so many other people lying next door, and next door to next door? Happy Christmas? You really want to, no? Darling?

I mumbled a few words into the night, enriching the air in my own way, as I would alone in my father's rice fields. There I used to imagine an embrace that would encompass the whole world: beyond the coconut trees, the chicken shed, the wild pigs, leopard and bear. But I had never imagined before the multitudes in a city, breathing their way into each other's lives like this.

Dias was a Christian like Nili. He wore a little cross on a thin gold chain around his neck. Maybe that was why he was so happy tonight. Maybe they gave each other much more when they shared knowledge as well as gifts. I wanted to know, was there something special between Christians at this time of year? Was it money?

Then I heard goodbyes and Mr Dias's old Wolseley start up and trundle out. I heard Mister Salgado go back inside the house. The party was over. He could call me now if he wanted to eat. My own hunger had passed for the moment.

Later, when I thought he must have gone to bed, I went into the main house to lock up and turn out the lights. Only the standard lamp in the sitting-room was on and the twinklers on the Christmas tree. I thought perhaps the Christmas lights could be left as this was a special night, but the lamp should be switched off. I walked in softly and suddenly saw them, Mister Salgado and Nili, on the sofa near the tree. They were huddled together, whispering. They didn't notice me. It was their Christmas. I retreated until I could hear them no more.

III

A Thousand Fingers

A FEW DAYS later Nili moved in. For us it was the beginning of a new era.

Mister Salgado didn't say anything about it to me, nothing at all about her or their plans. Yet another new minister was defending himself on the radio when I heard Mister Salgado drive out in his car—his blue Alfa Romeo, one of the first 1300s around. He came back a couple of hours later with Miss Nili in the front seat and two suitcases and some boxes in the back.

'Where to put them?' I asked.

'Take them inside,' he said. 'Nili-*nona* can have my room. Put my clothes in the other room.' He spoke confidently, in command.

'I'll be staying here now,' Nili added softly. 'With you.' She smiled.

I should have expected it, I suppose, but the speed at which our circumstances changed surprised me. I didn't let anything show. I nodded and quickly picked up the cases. It was not any of my business how they organized their affairs. I was pleased that she was coming to live with us; the whole place seemed to pick up the moment she stepped in.

Mister Salgado shut the door of the car and escorted Nili into the house. To see them like that you would think she had never been inside before. She walked so carefully.

I had cleaned the house early that morning. Saturday—and its lunar equivalent—used to be the most unpredictable day of the week for me. Sometimes Mister Salgado would ask me to come with him to the market because he had a yearning for bananas or pineapples or red meat, and needed me to identify the best buys for him. I had become his expert on these things. I had my own system for judging quality and could drive a much harder bargain than he could. But if he did take me with him like that, my housework got completely out of joint. Then it became a real rush to get everything done by the end of the day, and sometimes it didn't happen. Luckily that day he had gone off to his rendezvous by himself. So the sitting-room was swept and tidy for them when they came; and both Mister Salgado's bedroom and the spare room he now proposed to inhabit were pristine.

In the sitting-room Nili hesitated. I said 'Missy-*nona*, wait. I will go prepare the room.'

'Sit down,' Mister Salgado said to her. 'We can have some coffee.' She was still a guest; in that sense nothing had changed yet.

'Yes, Sir. I'll bring coffee.' I took the bags into the bedroom first. I put them down next to the bed; the prospect of moving all his things to the other room was not something to look forward to. And for what purpose? For how long? It was a man's room: should I change the furniture? My orange curtains? I remembered how she had looked out of the window the time we came in together to choose a shirt. Was this move in her mind even then?

When I brought the coffee I found the two of them sitting opposite each other as usual, staring. I put the tray with the two cups on the table between them. She didn't take sugar, only milk; it was enough to make my head spin to know that I knew that. I pushed one of the cups closer to her and she looked up at me, 'Thanks, Triton.'

I took in her words like honey. 'I'll go and get the room ready,' I said.

Something gurgled. I looked at Mister Salgado. He was smiling. He leaned back and his face seemed to relax into something much bigger than before. I didn't know what was so amusing. His shirt collar was twisted on one side as if he had been fingering it. I didn't do anything about it. I reckoned she could sort out things like that now. She could tell him, or lean over and straighten it if she wanted to. Perhaps she liked it like that: more casual, happy, reckless. He was a man's man once; now he had become a woman's man.

But the trouble was his shoes; the clothes I could fit into the almirah in the spare room, but Mister Salgado had too many shoes. He hoarded them. It didn't matter before because there was a shoe cupboard in his room which could take a lot of shoes. There were usually about ten pairs, including his brogues, in there at any one time; most of them too pointed ever to be comfortable. But the spare room did not cater for shoe hoarding. I couldn't leave them where they were because I knew Nili also went in for shoes in a big way. The boxes she had brought were probably all filled with shoes. Black, gold, ivory, high-heeled, flat-bottomed, cork-lined, rubber and leather shoes. Even red shoes. And sandals galore. I had seen her sandals: tan leather sandals with creaky filigree over the instep and sometimes even around the heel. She was keen on that sort of thing. Indian *chappals*, leather braids and solid plain slab-silver jewellery. In the end I dumped Mister Salgado's shoes into an old tea-chest and stored it on the back veranda, hoping they would not grow mildew and degenerate like all the rest of the junk of the house. The problem could be confronted later; perhaps we could get a second shoe-cupboard made. It would not be too expensive, not compared with the money he spent on his feet anyway.

After I shifted everything out and lined the shelves with new brown paper and freshened all the nooks and crannies with drops of Moorish rose-water, I considered the suitcases. They were not locked. I opened them. I had never touched women's clothes before: tie-dye batik blous-es, silky dresses in slippery bundles. With one hand I was able to lift a whole pile of thin shiny material; it was as light as feathers. Underneath I discovered little black pieces and white garments: satin cups with pointed ends where the seams met, coupled up with straps and hooks and bits of elastic. I picked another squidgy bundle up but felt that perhaps this was all getting a little out of hand. The material was like nothing I had ever come across before; not like Mister Salgado's underwear with pockets and pouches and little gaps for his pipe to shoot. His material was always sensible cotton, except for the jockstraps which seemed to be made of hard parchment. But Miss Nili's were out of this world. I went back and asked her what to do. 'The almirah is clear,' I said. 'Should I unpack the suitcases?'

'Oh yes, please. Just shove everything in wherever you can. It's only clothes.'

'In the boxes also?' Mister Salgado asked.

'No, leave the boxes for the moment. There's nothing there I really need.'

'Sir . . . ' for a moment my mouth tingled, 'the shoes.'

Mister Salgado recoiled.

'Another shoe-cupboard . . .'

He shook his head, I thought to say no, but he waved his hand meaning, *later, later.* We will discuss it later. The shoes were not as important as getting Nili properly settled. To my mind that was absolutely right: the blouses and slacks, dresses and bits of string and lace. I never realized a woman had so many shapes to get in and out of. And they all smelled different. From her skin? Her perfume? From inside her? One suitcase had a bag of dirty clothes including knickers stiffened in the middle with what seemed like dried milk; I put them in our laundry basket. I was surprised to find the dirty clothes but I guessed she had packed in a hurry. If you wear clothes the modern way you can't help but have a backlog of dirty pieces. For me it was a lot easier in those days: when my shirt and sarong got dirty I washed them straight away. There was no interim stage. Bucket and soap. But she had a different way of wearing clothes. I put the clean items away nice and neat, and stored the suitcases on top behind the carved faceboard.

*

MISTER SALGADO glowed as if a magic lantern were shining beneath his skin. His face would constantly break into a boyish smile, the corners of his mouth pulling up irresistibly, his teeth forcing themselves into the open air. The sharp angles of his face became more rounded; he seemed to thicken out and with every meal he shared with her in our house, he grew stronger. I expected his shirts to burst open at the seams, the muscles of his arms to stretch each thread a hundredfold. Even the house felt different when he was there; his presence was more discernible as it cut through Nili's lingering perfume. He looked at me when he spoke whereas before he had seemed to communicate through a box of mirrors and drum-skin. It felt as though he were really there, in front of me for the first time: not dreaming in some other place.

Miss Nili became the lady—our *nona*—of the house, but he never said anything about her, about her position. Something in the air in those heady days seemed to make for such unorthodox changes. The rest of the country, sliding into unparalleled debt, girded itself for change of a completely different order: a savage brutalizing whereby our *chandiyas*—our braggarts—would become thugs, our dissolutes turn into mercenaries and our leaders excel as small-time megalomaniacs. But in those days I had no real interest in the politics of the countryside: we each have to live by our own dreams. The changes in our house were momentous enough for me. Not only did the bedrooms change hands but furniture was moved in every room, plants were imported into bare corners, new batik-style curtains ordered, old chairs reupholstered; walls, woodwork, tats repainted. A lot of these things I had to organize myself, but it was simply a matter of following instructions. I didn't have to decide any of it; I didn't have to work out the timing and the priorities. Missy-*nona*, Nili, did all of that. It was not for nothing that she ran the front office at the Sea Hopper Hotel. But she left the kitchen and the cooking entirely to me; she took charge and by doing so allowed each of us to feel we were in charge of something too.

I wanted her to taste the whole world through my fingers so I cooked like a magician—tiger prawns to rum soufflés. I even cooked a beautiful parrot fish for her the first time he took her down to the beach house.

'Let's go skin-diving tomorrow,' he had said, 'down in my bay.'

'Isn't it dangerous . . . ?'

'It's a fabulous world. Fabulous. I'll show you the fish, the corals. We could look for turtles. Then float to the edge. Swim over the abyss!'

Nili raised her eyebrows. 'The abyss?'

'Beyond the reef it's a cliff. The floor plunges thousands of feet. The bottom of the world. You can't see it. Only all these prehistoric structures. Huge mountains rising up. But it's safe. Once you are out there you could drift to Indonesia and back. No problem.' Mister Salgado ran his fingers through his long hair, pulling at it.

'Abyss sounds so silly.'

'It's *not*.'

'Don't be so touchy.'

He moved closer to her and she reached out towards him. 'Underwater,' he said and lifted her up on her toes, pulling her close. 'You know? *Underwater*.' She laughed.

*

OUT BEYOND the reef, shoals of fish turned in a dazzle. Mister Salgado held Nili's hand while the sea-foam swirling below rubbed out their footprints as they walked along the sand. For once there was nobody else around— no urchins, no drifters—the beach was our own except at first for Wijetunga, Mister Salgado's assistant.

Wijetunga helped me unpack the foodstuffs in the kitchen. He had grown a thick beard. His hair was longer and he had developed a low parting on one side from which the hair was slicked over across to the other. He was more prepared to speak to me this time. The little boy who used to help him was not around. When I asked about the *kolla*, Wijetunga said he had sent him to school. 'A child must have education. Otherwise what will he become, here? In this country?' As he spoke his breathing became easier, as if something had cleared his nose and throat.

Later Mister Salgado came and asked him about his work. Wijetunga spoke with his head down. He said he had to go away that afternoon for a few days. He had sent a request about it to Colombo. He had not known we were coming. 'OK, OK,' Mister Salgado waved his hand about. 'That's fine. I can check the reports next week. You come to the office in Colombo. We can talk then, that will be better.' Mister Salgado seemed relieved.

Afterwards Wijetunga asked me, 'Why doesn't he come this side so much now? Not even a message for weeks. And then suddenly this trip. Why?'

I mentioned Miss Nili.

'But who is she?'

'Nili-*nona*,' I said. 'She runs a hotel for tourists in Colombo.'

'Tourists?' he shook his head in dismay. 'Listen, these people all think tourists will be our salvation. All they see is pockets full of foreign money. Coming by the plane-load. Don't they realize what will happen? They will ruin us. They will turn us all into servants. Sell our children . . . ' He gripped my shoulder hard. 'You know, brother, our country really needs to be cleansed, *radically*. There is no alternative. *We have to destroy in order to create.* Understand? Like the sea. Whatever it destroys, it uses to grow something better.' He let go of me and stared at the ocean turning itself inside out, a deep blue gathering to swallow the sun. 'Have you heard the Five Lessons?' he asked me softly. He didn't mean the scriptures—the Precepts. He meant the simplified lessons that explained the crisis of capitalism, the history of social movements and the future shape of a Lankan revolution. 'You know what happened in Cuba?'

I said, 'But I am only a cook.'

'We will have to talk more, brother, next time.' His beard opened, allowing a small injured smile out. 'You say nothing to him, all right? Not yet. For now, brother, you cook. But one day . . . ' he closed his eyes for a moment, 'we will be able to live for ourselves.' I wondered if he had ever spoken like this to anyone before. I took a deep breath, but the air had turned sour, blowing in over the copra pit at the edge of the compound.

*

THAT NIGHT by the ocean I made a *pol-kiri-badun* curry, a steamed *pittu* and my most special dish of brinjals, but Mister Salgado and Nili hardly noticed what I had done. The shiny purple skins were decorated with the green tomatoes and our sweet Embilipitiya grass, but I suppose a compliment would have been difficult to draw out there on our first night: they were so enamoured of each other.

After eating together they went out on the night beach. I imagined them with the moon in their hands, fingers enmeshed, picking their way over green turtle eggs, their ears filled with the roar of the surf, rubbed by the wind and salt and swelling up; their tongues wordlessly pricking into each other and enlivening their bodies; the ocean rushing up the sloping beach, snatching at their ankles with a thousand fingers and clawing the sand from under their feet.

Mister Salgado would be able to explain the exact ebb and flow of the whole cluster of galaxies at a time like this: how the light of the moon moved the tide, and heaven was reflected in the shape of our heads, and each exquisite sensation was lodged forever in the contours of a hypo-thetical mind. And how it all moved as the earth moves, the earth deep inside ourselves: the only *terra firma* in our tentative lives.

In my boxroom a mosquito discovered my ear and dug in. Each time I smacked it a smug drone would rise tri-umphantly out of my hurting head. I felt it pierce my skin; according to Mister Salgado, if you can feel the sting it is not the resurgent malaria that she is injecting in return for her suck, but I was not so sure. Then I heard Nili and Mister Salgado returning to the bungalow, enter-ing their room. A sandal—a leather *sereppu*—dropped on the concrete and was kicked slithering across the floor. The whole house seemed to creak and flap as the wind rose; the shutters shook. The confusion of sounds was too much. I couldn't bear to stay inside any longer and I went out to immerse myself in the simpler roar of the ocean and let it, like the waves, curl in my ears and overwhelm me.

In the morning, at first light, the sea lay like a Madras pancake. *Thosai* flat. Tranquil. As the other two were unlikely to get up for ages, I decided to walk the length of the beach. Further down the bay the fishing boats were coming in: thin, dark vessels with matchstick figures heading for home.

The wet sand hugged my bare foot at every step, sucking at the sole; the surf burbled under the surface and small crabs raced into their sand holes. After about a quarter of a mile I came to where the boats were drawn up. There was a line of big black outriggers on the dry sand. Another boat was coming in. Three men were hauling it up on to the beach: one pushing from the sea, the other two with their backs to each of the arched outrigger arms, digging their heels in the sand and using each surge of the sea.

> *'Ahey, ohoy, apa thenna,*
> *ahey, ahoy thel dhala . . . '*

With each rhyme they heaved, and the boat would slide an arm's length. By the time I reached them, the boat was over the hump of the white frothy beach on to dry sand. One man got up into the narrow top of the boat and started chucking the catch out. He threw a large blue-striped fish at my feet.

'What is it?' I had never seen such a brilliantly coloured one before.

'Fish!' the man laughed. He was straddling the boat with his sarong twisted into a loincloth.

I asked him where he got it.

He lifted his arm and pointed to the sea, 'Out there. We go to the mouth of the sea.' The edge of Mister Salgado's blue abyss.

'Was it good?'

'Last night it was not too good over there. We only got a couple of these and some stupid stray mackerel.'

The other two men came closer. One took his dirty green hat off and scratched his head. 'Sometimes, if we are in luck, we might catch a shark or something bigger. But you really need a Johnson motor to go far enough for that, beyond the reef, and be sure of getting back in time.'

'Sometimes we go all night and there's nothing. Not like in the old days when they used to fly into our hands.'

I was surprised. 'Nothing?'

'These days the fish are not plentiful.'

'Why?'

'What do you expect with this government?' they hooted, laughing.

The blue-striped creature wriggled and flopped over, coating both its sides in seasoned sand. I wondered how long it would take to die. Before cooking it I would have to wash it and gut it; scrape off the scales but keep the colour. There were blurry yellow stripes as well as blue. The mouth was a hard beak of triangular pincers.

'How much?' I asked nodding at it. I thought Nili would be impressed.

I think they thought I was a real city *mahathaya* because when I got my money out, one of the men said he would clean the fish for me. I didn't even have a purse;

just a couple of notes in my shirt pocket. I liked the idea of them thinking of me like that, it was worth the extra money. They threw the guts back into the sea as if to feed the waves.

I retraced my vanished steps thinking all the time of how I should cook the fish. I had no idea what it would taste like. Maybe the colour was not a camouflage for protecting its flesh but an enticement to distract from its awful taste. My best bet, I reckoned, was to steam it, and put plenty of lime in the sauce. Grilling would destroy the magic of its colours and the point of it all.

When I got back I found Nili sitting by a tree, playing with her hair, lifting it up and letting it drop on her curved back. She smiled dreamily at me. 'What a wonderful place, no?'

After breakfast, I sat and stared at the sea. A beach house requires very little day-to-day housework. The sand gets everywhere whatever you do. It was a holiday, in a way, for me also.

Later she came to watch me in the kitchen. She peered over my shoulder at the fried rice: 'Hmm, that smells lovely.'

'*Temperadu,*' I explained. Then I showed the fish all ready for the steam boat.

'What amazing colours!'

I couldn't stop myself from smiling.

'You got this on the beach?'

'From the fishermen,' I explained.

She called out to Mister Salgado, 'Come and look at what Triton has got.'

He came up. 'What?'

'Look at this blue fish.'

'Parrot fish,' he said. 'A bit of an acquired taste. Coral crunchers. If only you'd come snorkelling, I'd show you.' I felt all jittery and weak. 'Very pretty though. I'm sure Triton will make it tasty.'

I was on tenterhooks for the next hour until they had finished lunch. I had to conjure up some chilli *sambol* and sweeten the lime sauce invoking all the godlings of fish-cooking in all the poky kitchens of Southern China to produce a favourable result. Fortunately it worked out. Whatever taste the flesh might have had, the Chinese sauce disguised it. Nili was still smiling at the end of the meal, and Mister Salgado was happy cooling off with a beer. He fell asleep in an armchair and Nili chatted to me for a while.

She said the sea looked too rough for reef-combing, but that she would like to see the fish catch the next morning. I said I would take her. We didn't have to go as early as I had done because the fishermen had told me about the market in the town. She could lie in, I said, if she wanted to.

*

THE SUN was already burning when we got to the market in the morning. The clammy stench of fresh fish blood, guts, bile and brine cooking in the magnified heat rolled down the dusty road to greet us. I walked slightly behind Nili: guide, protector and entourage. 'Here, this way,' I said leaning forward to point the way. Vendors shrieked and shouted inside the grey stone market hall. The entrance was a narrow, dark doorway plastered with subversive slogans and posters celebrating the land of the lion. It led to a large, shallow square open to the sky. Step-like ledges rose up on all sides to a covered Roman gallery. The arena in the middle was where the bigger sea-creatures were butchered. We almost stepped on a huge mottled ray camouflaged against the gritty wet concrete floor. Nili saw its eye on the floor and started. She pulled me to stop me from treading on it. The head was like the gigantic hood of a snake. At the other end of the hall someone shouted, *'Mora!'* and a small crowd gathered around. Some carried newspapers and umbrellas, others little parcels of fish. There was a terrific thrashing on the ground and I saw the fat, grey body of a reef shark twisting as a fishmonger hacked at it with a cleaver. Blood spurted. The creature flapped and writhed. The man brought the cleaver shining down again and again like a hammer. Smart, fat thunks punctuated by the sharper sound of the blade sparking off the concrete beyond the shark's beady eyes. It did not die until the head had been severed, and the man stood up with its curved slit of teeth smiling in his hand. Thick, black blood pumped out of the body on the floor, forming a pool. Someone chucked a bucket of water and washed it into the gully. I looked at Nili. She was holding her stomach, her face drawn tight.

We walked along the gallery and I pointed out the fish neatly arranged in rows on wooden tables. Their eyes like buttons and their mouths wide open in 'O's of surprise at being lifted from the sea, gagging and drowning on a moon of warm air, their stomachs turning before being ripped open and gutted. 'Fish, crab, lobster?' I asked her. 'Which to buy?'

Crabs and crayfish were heaped in baskets, waiting to be plunged into boiling water. I used to think these bone-heads cursed their killers as the air hissed through their crusty joints, but they feel nothing and would break your finger given half a chance. Nili was fascinated by them. 'These,' she said, pointing at the crayfish. I bought three trussed up with coconut fronds. I don't think she had ever been to a fish market before, at least not one as raw as this. I suppose she never had reason to.

There was a rush of excitement across the hall. 'What's happening?' Nili asked.

'Someone has caught a dolphin,' the crab-seller said.

'They got a dolphin?'

'Yes, they will kill it quickly. Very good money. Someone's lucky day.'

'Let's go,' Nili said and pulled my arm. 'I want to go back now.'

'It happens,' I told her. 'They have to make a living.'

'Killing . . . ' she shook her head to herself. 'Why dolphins? What next?'

Outside a man was filling an unmarked van with baskets of dead fish. Small pieces of bleached white coral marked the municipal parking lot.

*

SOON AFTER that, back in town, Nili gave up her job. She said it was time to start thinking of her own hotel. But instead she and Mister Salgado spent all their time in his— now their—room, or visiting friends, nightclubs, even restaurants to eat other people's food. Mister Salgado's coastal project passed its zenith; he should have been drawing his conclusions together in some big report but, rather than analysing and writing, he procrastinated. From time to time he would ask Wijetunga to produce more data, but he never studied the results. He would occasionally bring a batch of papers home and go into his study. But then he would wander out to 'take air'. He would see her on the veranda and forget to go back in. She brought out the urban socialite in him and shrouded the scholar. It was not something deliberate on her part; simply a desire in him.

Meanwhile a nationwide concern for *inland* seas grew as politicians invoked the spurious visions of ancient kings. All our engineers, trained in London and New England, suddenly saw great advantages in reviving the traditional skills of irrigation. But Mister Salgado let all their machinations pass in a haze. None of it mattered to him then.

Sometimes in the evening, when I served my home cooking, they would talk of the Blue Lagoon or the Pink Barracuda and how they must go there; or when was it somebody or other was due to meet them there, or elsewhere. I heard about baked crab during one of these conversations. Nili had loved the breadcrumbs on top and the mixture of crab-meat and cheese inside—the speciality of some *nouveau*-chef who had been to the new hotel school. I could not believe that was all there was to it: I wanted to ask for more details but Mister Salgado said, 'Triton can make some.'

'He won't know how to make that?'

I was stunned to hear her say I could not. By then I thought I had shown my versatility, the infinite range of my skill, if only she had just a little faith. But she sounded so convinced that baked crab was beyond me that I despaired of ever proving my worth. I could not understand it. I wished I could turn myself inside out and start all over again. I wished I knew more about people, women like her.

'Bake the whole crab?' I asked.

'Just the body.' Mister Salgado looked at her. 'The shell stuffed with all the meat from the claws and the legs. You take everything out, mix it up, and then stuff it.'

'Stuff it?'

Nili cupped a hand and poked the hole she made out of it with her other hand. 'Yes, stuff it, Triton, with onion and parsley and cheddar cheese, you know, stuff it.'

'And crab?' I said, already imagining half a teaspoon of black pepper, a pinch of ground cinnamon and fresh, chopped green coriander. Lemon and a dash of brandy from the bottle Mister Salgado got at Christmas from Professor Dunstable would make it exceptional and, I was sure, better than she had ever had at some stuffy hotel restaurant. 'Yes, can do. No problem. Tomorrow?' Deep inside the stuffing I would bury a seeded slice of green chilli steeped in virgin coconut oil.

She looked at me and smiled sweetly. 'Not tomorrow, Triton. There is a party tomorrow night. We will be out.'

I shrugged. 'Any time, say please.'

They went out to so many parties that I lost count. But this party turned out to be something more important: the inauguration of the era of the Mahaweli Scheme. A giant leap into inland irrigation not seen for a thousand years. The diversion of the biggest river in the land. The next day the two of them seemed to spend the whole afternoon preparing for the party.

'Everyone will be there!' he told her. It was the biggest since the government restricted the size of social parties to two hundred guests, our most telling measure of austerity.

'I know. This Minister everyone talks about so much is guest of honour, no? That's why it is so big. What should I wear? What do you want me to wear?'

'I don't know.' He looked worried. He was not looking forward to it, I think.

'That Benares silk? The purple one?' But purple was not her colour. I could tell her that. And Indian silk, on the rare occasions I had seen her in it, made her look like a bundle of Pettah cloth. It was too pompous for her skinny frame.

He said nothing.

'Are you sure I am invited?'

'Yes, darling, yes.'

'What did they say?'

'They said you were invited.'

'Me? Are you sure? Or is it for *wives?*'

He looked down at his shoes. There was a crack on the left one where the sole was sewn on. 'They said to bring you.'

'You think it won't look good. Yet another sign of your depravity is it? I am not a pedigree bitch, is that it? When it comes down to it, not good enough? Won't they like a bit of flair . . . '

'Hey, I want you to come. Wear anything. Purple is fine. Or that other thing. Wear whatever . . . I've got to get a new pair of shoes.'

While he went to the shops, I did the ironing. I had to iron everything, and she must have tried it all piece by piece in front of the long mirror in the bedroom. Occasionally I could hear it complain as she swivelled it on its round, wooden pivoty-spigot. It could catch the light from outside, and if she adjusted it properly she could see how her clothes flared from top to bottom. By about five o'clock I was bringing the clothes and leaving them on the hall-table outside her door every five minutes or so. She must have been sweating like a pig the rate she was changing. The bedroom was hot in the afternoon because the sun fell straight into it. The windows could catch a good breeze, but she had closed them to stop the new batik curtains blowing open and revealing her body to the prying eyes of house sparrows and cock-eyed mynah birds.

In the end I knocked on the door and asked whether she would like a cup of tea.

'Yes,' she hissed, struggling into yet another tight, skin-sucking garment on the other side of the wooden door.

When I brought the tea a little later, she opened the door for me. She was in Mister Salgado's red dressing-gown. There was a sheen to her face as if she had bathed and not yet dried herself, even though neither the bath nor the shower had been running. She was slightly breathless, her nose fat with drawing hot air; she smiled at me, widening her nostrils even more. The moisture rose from inside her and broke beautifully through her skin into heavy swollen drops. 'Just what I need,' she said taking the cup. Behind her I could see clothes in little coloured pats all over the place. The bed and chair festooned with silk. A bit of black lace showed by the lapel of the dressing-gown. Her sweat smelled sweet, ripe.

'Shall I bring something else?' I asked.

She laughed. 'No, I will have my tea and then get ready. This is such a stupid business.'

Mister Salgado came back a little later with his new shoes wrapped in newspaper. He went into the bedroom with her and after a while came out frowning and asked me to lay his own things out in the other room, his dressing-room.

When they eventually drove out that night they looked quite the glittering pair: Nili in turquoise with huge silver earrings dangling from her ears; Mister Salgado in a pale grey nationalistic tunic over dark trousers and his new black shoes.

As Mister Salgado's car gurgled down the drive into our deep unlit lane, I had a feeling inside me of everything sliding away, out of reach, into some other world.

*

THEY HAD not said where the party was but I imagined Mister Salgado and Nili out on some terrace by the sea, dancing the cha-cha-cha or the *kukul-kakul* wiggle. The band playing like they do on our old records. A brown and white dog sitting by the stage and peering into a brass horn, the waves crashing out on the beach, Mister Salgado's crushed coral sand churning, and their feet tracing a complicated pattern across a polished tiled floor. Lights strung across coconut trees would twinkle like stars and waiters would serve lobster tails, prawn *vadai* and devilled eggs on silver trays as big as the moon. I began to wonder what it would have been like if I had gone to work in a restaurant from the beginning, or gone to hotel school as he had once suggested. To have been right at the centre of events rather than having always to imagine. There seemed to be more of a future in an institution, I thought in my innocence then, than being in a house; but one has to take these things as they come. Maybe it was better to be able to sit on our front steps and imagine the prawn *vadai* I would flambé for those glitzy ladies with puce lips, than to be there having my bare feet pierced by their stiletto heels, being bossed and harried all night long without even a moment to think what the hell is it all about. It is hard enough to think anywhere. The garden was full of shadows, and the wretched hounds at number ten were barking. But what if Nili managed a restaurant and I was in charge of the kitchens . . . ?

It was past midnight when they finally came home. She was driving. The blue Alfa rolled to a stop right at the edge of the porch. She switched off the headlights and then the engine. She got out first and walked over to the other side and opened his door.

'Come on, we are home.'

'You drove?' He sounded sleepy and surprised.

'What do you think?'

'What happened to the driver?'

'How long has this been going on . . . ?' she sang softly.

'It's a good thing we don't have a driver, you know.' He shook a long straight finger at her. 'Did you hear what happened to Bala?'

'Come on, let's go in.'

'Bala came to his car and this fellow, his bloody driver, pulled a knife on him. Why did he do that? He cut him. He went for the throat. Helluva fight. Why did the bugger attack Bala?'

'I don't know, let's go. Come on.' She pulled him by an arm and almost toppled over herself. 'Come on, you said you wanted to make love, no?'

He hauled himself awkwardly out of the car and hobbled holding on to her. I didn't come out, even though both of them looked unsteady. I stayed in the shadows. 'Bala's grown a beard now. Terrified of shaving. Looks like that Che Guevara fellow.' They went through towards the bedroom. 'That Wijetunga on the beach also has grown one, did you see? Bloody beards everywhere.' I heard him slump down and Miss Nili swear softly. A little later she peered out.

'Missy?'

'Bring some water for me, Triton.'

I got her a glass of cold, filtered water. When I went back to my kitchen I heard her put a record on in the sitting-room. Music pulsed through the house. When the tune was over, someone turned a light out in the house next door. The garden turned darker, the music more sultry. I wanted to see what was going on.

I picked a pair of yellow towels out of the linen cupboard and went in. The record-player clicked to another disc. A song about a big brass bed. I peeped into the bedroom. Mister Salgado was snoring softly on the bed. He had taken his tunic off and undone his trousers, but he still had his shoes on with the laces dangling. The bedside light was on. Miss Nili was nowhere to be seen. I went over to the bathroom and quietly opened the door. She was standing by the bath: one leg raised, her foot on the edge of the bath; she was dabbing herself with a small pink flannel. Her clothes were piled on a chair. She was completely naked. She moved her head sideways and tucked her hair back behind her ear. I could see her nipples; her breasts were like faint ring marks. I could see her ribs, her small round stomach. Dimples. She looked up and I felt I was going to burst. I dropped the towels on the wicker basket by the door and ran back to my room.

My chest hurt. She had said nothing. She must have seen me standing there staring at her, yet she had said nothing. The blood pumping inside made me deaf.

I waited in my room. I don't know what I thought would happen, but it was the only thing I could do. From time to time I heard sounds as though someone was coming. But after a while I couldn't really tell what was happening. I tried to retrace all my steps in my mind but I could not. And yet I could see her naked body distinctly. It was as if it were next to me, looming closer.

*

ONE MORNING Robert, our Christmas guest, arrived with another woman in a taxi. He wore short trousers and sunglasses.

I opened the gate. He asked to see Mister Salgado. I said he had gone to the sea-front to do his calisthenics. 'OK, we'll wait,' Robert said and grinned politely. I seated them in the front bay, and the woman started to explain something to him. He clicked his head like a bird looking around, examining a new world. Miss Nili, who was not yet dressed, heard them and called for me. She asked who had come. I said it was the American gentleman from Christmas-time. I said he looked like a film-star.

'American film-star?'

I nodded. 'And he has a lady with him I have never seen before.'

'Oh yes?' She went out wearing only her black-and-white kimono, her freshly shaved legs glistening. 'Missy,' I said, but she didn't take any notice.

'Hello,' she greeted them, her body pressed against the doorway.

The woman looked up and smiled nervously. Robert jumped from his chair. 'Hi,' he said. 'We were hoping to see Ranjan.'

'Why? He wasn't expecting you.'

'I wasn't expecting *you!*'

'So, you want only to speak to him?'

'Doing some research, that's all. If I had known you'd be here . . . '

'Research on what?'

Robert grinned and nodded at his companion. 'Sujie would love to meet him. I told her he was *the* expert on the south coast. *The* authority.'

'So?' Miss Nili wrapped her arms around herself, nursing her round shoulders in the cups of her hands.

'Sujie is a journalist. She wants to do a story.'

The woman nodded but kept her eyes fastened on Miss Nili.

'Sit down.' She shrugged. 'Sit, sit. Triton will bring some tea.'

'Have you lime juice? Or maybe a beer? Something cool would be nice.' Robert settled back into the easy chair. His legs had hefty, awkward muscles like squashed snakes coiled under his skin, and his toes looked as though they had been stubbed on concrete streets, the flesh puffed around the tiny nails. He sat with his feet pointed on the floor.

I had only one lime left in the kitchen; fortunately there was an old bottle of lemonade at the back of the fridge. Mister Salgado had opened it to make some new citrus cocktail he had read about. It was flat but cold. I put some ice in the glass and took it out with some tea for the other two. Miss Nili had sat down with them and was listening to Robert spouting about village life and the next General Election.

I placed his iced glass on the table next to him. He didn't look at me, he was so busy with the story he was feeding Miss Nili. She was only half listening to what he was saying; she was studying the other woman, the journalist, who seemed lost in wonder at my carefully brewed up-country tea sent direct from the factory by Mister Salgado's cousin. She was staring at the cup as if she had never seen tea before. Her soft, black, straight hair spread over her forehead and seemed to fall into her shiny dog-eyes, but she did not brush it away; her head itself was sunk into her plump shoulders, and she gripped her cup with both hands. Maybe that was the way a real reporter got to the heart of a story. I noticed she did have a note-book—a rolled-up, blue school exercise book—stuck in her bag with a yellow Biro clipped to it. What did she jot down? When? And how was it transformed into *news*?

'You are a reporter?' Miss Nili asked her when Robert paused to draw breath.

The woman looked up, surprised. 'Yes, I mean no, a journalist. Now I do features.' She gave the name of a weekly magazine. The corners of Nili's lips twitched as if she wanted to smile. She looked at her for a long time.

Robert jiggled his ice and said, 'Great house this. Very nice.'

'What feature are you doing?' She spoke to the other woman again, ignoring Robert.

'Actually, I am not sure yet, but Robert here says I should meet some people who know about the coast area, and we were told to talk to Ranjan Salgado. So we are here. Really, I am in Robert's hands, you know.' She looked appealingly at Robert, but he had closed his eyes for a moment. His head was right back. He had two small bald patches in his beard just above his throat as if he had been bitten.

'I see.'

He opened his eyes and looked straight at Nili. 'Well, you know, there's a lot happening here that nobody understands very much about. I reckon there are some serious lessons to be learned from observing behaviour in this extraordinary, I reckon, deeply *erotic* country . . . ' He grinned again.

'You have come to do this?'

'Sure.'

'How good of you.'

'I mean, have you seen that dancing down the coast? Out of this world. So uninhibited. Really wild.'

Then Mister Salgado beeped the horn at the gate, and I went to open it. 'Some people, Sir,' I said. 'That Robert-*mahathaya* and a lady from the newspapers have come to see you.'

'Who?' He looked at me suspiciously.

'They want to talk to you, Sir. About the sea.'

He eased the car under the portico.

Robert jumped to his feet again when Mister Salgado came up the steps. 'Nice wheels,' he said. His companion's cup rattled on its saucer, splashing some of the tea. 'Sorry, sorry,' she said quietly to the cup.

Mister Salgado looked disapprovingly at Nili in her kimono; she tugged at the lapels and said, 'Robert has brought his friend to talk to you.'

The journalist lady offered her hand. 'Heard so much about you, it's a pleasure to meet you.'

'Oh really?'

'Yes, we wanted to talk to you about the south coast. About what you think. It would be really great to get your expert views. A real help.'

'What exactly do you want to know?'

She pushed back her hair and looked at Robert; 'Well, to put it simply—in a nutshell—how do you think the lifestyle in coastal villages is changing as a result of this sea-erosion?'

Robert leaned forward. 'You reckon the sea is coming in, is that right?'

Miss Nili got up, 'I'll leave you to your erotic sea,' she said and went inside.

Mister Salgado watched her disappear. She was bare-foot. 'What?'

Robert was also watching her. 'Erosion. Sea-erosion,' he said quickly. 'You said the sea will reduce the size of the beaches on the south coast. We want to know, has it happened? How much? Has it already changed the way of life in the villages?'

Mister Salgado was frowning. Something inside his skull pulled his face in; it completely absorbed him. The other two sat and waited. After a moment he sighed. 'Look, we are doing a simple project. My fellows have written some papers on it; the equilibrium of water and the effects of human muck on polyp life. You should go and read them. We haven't put any villages, any people, under a microscope. I am sure their way of life has changed. Maybe because the sea is rising. But maybe because Armstrong kicked the moon. Or because someone in Brazil has invented the perfect plastic bag, or maybe even because some Lumumba revolutionaries are talking about the price of fish. I don't know. What changed your life? Sunspots?' He looked at Robert.

'OK, OK. A lot of things. Yeah, I understand. A lot of things change. But we thought maybe you could isolate a factor. Just maybe?'

'You go down to the Ministry. Those chaps in there say they know everything. They can help you. Not me. Not us.' Mister Salgado was upset. It made him unapproach-able. I had learned early on to let him be when he was upset and in a bad mood. There was no way of knowing what was going on with him. Eventually the mood would wear off; he would work his way through it. Then given a good meal, a glass of beer, life would be back to normal.

But it takes time, years, to learn how other people cope with themselves, how they come to terms with the changes that happen, always happen around them.

*

To Miss Nili's coterie of friends, she and Mister Salgado were a daring example of a real modern couple: in love, independent and carefree. They were *cool.* More hedonistic than the latest Zeffirelli film—*Romeo and Juliet.* An appealing contrast to the despondency of a nation grappling with the dilemmas of uneconomic development. Instead of an extended family, we grew a network of admirers, oglers and hangers-on. They craved my cooking. If I were cooking for two, I would soon be cooking for half-a-dozen. They kept coming, hankering after our food and eager to see how long the romance would last. None of them, not Danton Chidambaram the lawyer, nor Vina who had started a batik boutique, nor her boyfriend Adonis with his fluorescent motorbike, nor Sarina who wanted to be a model, nor Jay, nor Gomes, nor Susil Gunawardene ever gave anything in return. None of them, except dear Dias who would have given his life if it were his to give, would ever offer anything. They would drop by in threes or fours all the time, and by the end of the week—*poya* or no *poya*—they would invade in shoals. Mister Salgado let them come and learned to greet them— her crowd—with a cool beer and an indulgent smile. He learned to enjoy their wanton adulation, even though the socializing seemed to be wearing the time he had together with Nili very thin. Then in April that year Palitha Aluthgoda was killed.

He was the boss of one of the biggest private companies in the island. He had a mansion down by the cemetery. I had never seen him, but everybody knew of him. Palitha Aluthgoda had led a fabulous life. He was a Nugegoda man who started out as nothing more than a fitter in a motor garage near the Eye Hospital. But he was smart. He wheeled his way into the transport business and then, through some uncle of his in the ruling party, set up a lucrative import–export business and made money hand over fist. He became the country's most flamboyant millionaire. He had everything, at a time when most people had nothing. Then one sunny day, when he stopped his white Mercedes by the Dehiwela bridge and called out to an ice-cream vendor to bring an ice *palam* for his new paramour, the vendor pulled out a gun and blasted him. Two nine millimetre bullets burst his eyes; his face was blown apart. People all around were screaming and there were ice *palams* and icy-chocs all over the place, melting in the sun. The killer sped away on his cycle. It was big news. Nobody had believed such a thing could happen. Those were the days; people felt real shock. The death was monumental: it made the front page of all the newspapers. And the story of the killing, the rumours of love nests, jealousy, communist plots, necromancy, poor company dividends and mysterious cosmic justice flew around the whole country and buzzed into our house where we had the usual gathering.

Dias came over with a clutch of stories rolled up in his newspaper. 'I-say-you-know-what-*men*, have you heard the news? How do you like that? Aluthgoda shot with a Bren gun!'

'What, *men*? What?'

'He had it coming. You can't screw everyone like he did without getting screwed yourself one day.' Danton Chidambaram's moustache squirmed with delight at the elegance of his own analysis.

But Jay, a young, prematurely balding man who often talked of the brotherhood of mankind, disagreed. 'It's not all that money-making, *men*, I'll tell you what it was: all this flamboyant bloody lifestyle. Spending like there's no tomorrow, as if nobody cared. You know, living like a lord while the rest of us have to tighten our belts . . . '

'Conspicuous consumption,' someone whispered.

Vina raised her blue-shadowed eyes towards heaven. 'I knew he would get bumped off. A bullet was coming his way from the day he was born. That bitch of his came so many times to the shop, but never bought anything from me. Always *ooing* and *aaing*, pulling everything out, but in the end they put some excuse about the colour or something . . . I don't know how this talk of flamboyant ever started, they never spent a cent in my shop!'

'But to be killed like that? With a gun? *Sten* gun, no? In broad daylight? How can that happen? What the hell is going on?' Gomes was a Radio Ceylon man, continuously flabbergasted by everything around him. He could only speak in a tone of high-pitched incredulity.

Jay shook his head disgustedly, '*Chi!* This country will end up like a bloody banana republic.'

'No, no, no, no,' Dias bubbled. 'After all, what about SWRD? Old Bandaranaike? Now *his* assassination was a real first. Nowhere else in the world had anything like that happened. Even before Kennedy we had a real modern assassination. *Assassination*, you know. It was a bad show killing the Prime Minister like that but you have to hand it to our fellows, they know how to do these things. We are not that backward. And where else have you got a bloody monk doing it? You'd think people would use the trick more often, you know. A monk's robe is the perfect disguise. You see, in your *hamudurova* robe you can hide even a bazooka and stand there. Everybody will kowtow and pass by assuming you are contemplating nirvana. All you do is stand still and look at some plantain leaf or whatever with a long face.'

'Only hold the barrel pointing down, huh,' Adonis stood up to demonstrate, his arm jerking between his thighs.

'*Chi*, Adonis! Stop it.' Vina slapped his bottom.

'Anything,' Dias went on, 'you just bide your time. No one bothers you. All you need is to shave your head, and pronto you get there . . . any place. Even nowadays.'

'But why? Why did Aluthgoda get it in the neck?' Gomes butted in.

'I say, it was the face, *men*.'

'But why?'

'That is what everybody is asking.'

'He had an empire, no? Do you think he was trying to take over the ice-cream company?'

Dias spread out his newspaper. 'Everyone has a theory.'

Only Nili was calm. 'But he made a very bad name the way he was living. It's a real shame. This country deserves better. Some decent men, not these crooks . . .'

Sarina, who liked to copy everything Nili did, nodded. 'It had to happen. This is exactly what happens when the *have-nots* see the *haves* having so much.' She was looking at Vina's Adonis while she spoke. He had sat down and had picked up Vina's hand and was slowly sucking her fingers.

'If you are right and it is the money-making that brought this on, capitalism's death, then I would have thought it would be that partner of his, Mahendran, who would be first. You know, the students say Indians like him are the Fifth Column.' Jay droned on like a schoolmaster. 'Business first, then the army comes. It is completely the opposite of the Alexandrian method of empire-building. It is the Asian style, true, no?'

'Anglo-Asian!'

'So you believe in all this Indian expansionism?'

'Why not?' Jay's shining head tilted. 'But what about their Naxalites?'

'Naxa-whats, *men*? Just look at the numbers. The demography is what will drive the politics. Always has. Hundreds of millions bubbling away . . . like China.'

When Mister Salgado spoke he sounded very sombre. He echoed Nili's sentiments, 'All I know is that it is a bad business. This kind of thing is very bad.'

For a moment the chattering stopped. The warm air rumbled with the distant sound of a train and the sea, the wind in the trees.

A few weeks later the big man and his death disappeared from everyone's thoughts. Palitha Aluthgoda, after all his efforts at making a big name for himself, ended up being remembered only for the manner of his death. The work of his assassin—some unknown guerrilla—became the more enduring achievement.

*

'LET'S EAT out tonight,' Miss Nili said. 'That new place near the park, let's go there.'

'But we went out last night!'

'So?'

'Triton can get us some crabs instead. Or prawns. We could ask Dias and Tippy to come and have a party.'

'I'm tired of those two. All they ever do is talk about racing or poker.'

'But Dias doesn't. He's a good fellow.'

'I like Dias, but that Tippy. I don't know what you see in him. He's a bad influence on the whole lot of you.'

Mister Salgado laughed. Tippy was one of Mister Salgado's own friends. He had come back recently from America with a beer-gut and an addiction to cards—especially poker, which at that time nobody else knew how to play. He had got a group together and taught them the game. He told them stories of Las Vegas and slot machines and the big money that hung on chance: fantasies that no one could resist. After a few beers their two-cent stakes would grow into bleary rupee chips, but by the end of the session, late at a weekend, it was always Tippy who walked away with the loot.

How the hell does he do it? his friends would ask.

Dias was his great supporter. 'He learned it from the maestros in the States, *men*. The *United* States.'

Nili thought Tippy was just a cheat. She also didn't like the way he flirted with her. He thought that he was a great charmer and that his sojourn in America had given him charisma, but she said that all he had gained was an inflated sense of his own worth. A beer-gut full.

'He is an authority on grain, you know,' Mister Salgado said. 'He studied in Ohio.'

'He can eat all right.'

'But for a country like ours he has real expertise. We need that. We need to grow our own food, otherwise how can we survive? Tippy carries a lot of weight. The Ministry of Agriculture people want him to do a big job.'

'All fat.' Nili pulled a face. 'Hot air and fat. He thinks every woman wants to bounce on his belly.'

Mister Salgado laughed. 'You know why he is called Tippy?' She made another grim face. 'Danton says it is because his foreskin doesn't quite reach the tip of his . . . '

'That Danton is as bad. What does he know?'

'They were at college together.' Mister Salgado laughed again. 'Anyway, there is a poker game due.'

'So?'

'I thought we could have it here, a party. Triton can do a crab curry.'

She snorted. 'For them? No way. I wouldn't waste good crab on that lot, and anyway I don't want to spend the whole day and night with you in a poker game, drinking. I want to go out.'

'But it's a regular game.'

'It's too regular. It's a waste of time.' She shook her head. 'You could be doing something.'

'What? I am doing something. I am doing something all the time but I need more data before I can do any more on the report. Meanwhile, let's play some cards instead of just chattering with your crowd. I don't complain about them do I? Why, even your friend Gomes plays. There's nothing wrong with a game.' He looked at her, baffled. 'Playing cards is a part of normal life. People have been doing it for centuries.' He folded his arms across his chest. 'Actually, you know, since at least the seventeenth century! True, in India.'

'That's stupid.'

They compromised: they would go out to dinner alone that night but have a poker-party at the weekend. Without crabs. I would have preferred it to have worked out the other way; in retrospect Mister Salgado would have as well.

For the poker lunch I made the usual yellow rice and chicken curry. As Tippy was coming, I made two extra measures of rice to make sure the dish was not cleaned out. Mister Salgado brought home two scrawny chickens with heads bigger than their legs. I was tempted to dice the birds to make the flesh go further, but it might have ended up nothing but bone then; it would have been too risky. Instead I made the sauce thick and doubled the chilli. The hotter the better: if not the meat then let the chilli be the challenge. They could all suck their teeth and wag their smart tongues and perspire. *Triton, this is really hot!* they would say. *Hotty hot, wow. Blows my mind, man!* Tippy would wink, *Currylingus, machang.*

Miss Nili was in a bad mood from the moment she woke up that morning. I could feel it through the bed-room door. When I placed the tea-tray on the table out-side, I could hear her whimpering through the bed sheets like a child coming out of a bad dream. A sound that seemed to come out of her head, some distant past, rather than the deep raw throat that her voice normally rippled out of. The bed creaked as she, or Mister Salgado, turned.

She had breakfast alone on the veranda outside the bedroom after Mister Salgado had gone to the shops. I brought her the usual slice of pawpaw, ripe and ready, cleaned of its black seeds and rocking in its self-made

cradle of yellowing skin with two half-moon limes balanced on hand-carved brown cocktail sticks. She squeezed
the lime on the raw flesh and then licked her fingers. She
stroked her throat, as if she were massaging lime juice into
the skin. I wondered whether she had ever squeezed a
whole lime, drop by drop, between her small breasts and
let the sour moisture run down her skin. What did they
do with the mango-stone I sometimes found in their bedroom in the morning? All chewed up and wasted; rubbed
out like a rock smoothed in a desert, or a gift passed from
one to the other over and over again, mouth to mouth.
Mango for the skin? A body tonic? For the lips? A lubric-
ant for them to live to the full the life of man and woman,
or some weird object of shared desire? She sat with her
legs tucked under her, stirring tea as if she were digging a
hole through the cup and saucer. Through the table, the
floor, down to the bowels of the earth.

'Missy,' I said, 'how about some special Rice Krispies?'

She glowered at me; her thin, carefully plucked eyebrows descending on her smooth wide forehead.

I picked up the empty cup from the table and waited
for a command, but she said nothing. 'Egg? Fried?
Scrambled?' I tried everything. 'Or omelette, with green
chilli and onion? A little butter?'

Later I saw her in the garden. She was poking around
with a cane, crushing the eggshells I had put in the
anthurium pots. Two crows cackled at her from the garden wall, and a cyclist going down the lane tinkled his
bicycle bell. She didn't even look up. Then she snapped
the cane and chucked it at the crows. As they rose up off
the wall I heard her shoo them, which only served to
make them caw louder and set off a chain reaction down

the trees and parapets of the whole neighbourhood. It was probably the noise of the crows more than anything else that eventually drove her back into the house. 'Bring a big bucket of boiling water, Triton. A big bucket.'

'Where?'

'Bring it out on the veranda.' She asked me to bring it when it was half full but to keep more water on the boil.

'Put it over here.' She pointed to the reed squares in front of a wooden stool she had strategically placed. I lowered the bucket to the ground. She smiled for the first time that morning, 'Thank you, Triton. Bring some more in about ten minutes.' She shook a few drops of rose-water from a small blue bottle in her hand and then, draping a blanket over her shoulders, she sat down in front of the bucket. 'It's called a sauna, Triton.' She slipped off her kimono under the blanket and dropped it on the cold floor. I picked it up. 'Ten minutes,' she said and ducked her head under the blanket making a steamy tent.

When I came back with a fresh bucket of hot water she popped her head out. Her face was wet and shiny and her eyes bright. She looked surprisingly alive. She opened the blanket briefly letting the damp hot air out and moved back. 'Pour it in.'

I bent by her feet and carefully poured the water in a steady stream making sure not to splash her legs. I could see the veins thicken down by her ankles. The steam made me sweat.

'That's it,' she moved in quickly and encased the steam and bucket again. 'One more,' she said from under the damp blanket. There was a little pool of water, or sweat, on the floor behind her. She had let the tats down, making the alcove close and humid. The whole place had the ambience of madness: like some hot-water shrine of a demonic sect.

Mister Salgado stopped me as I came back with the last bucketful. He looked at me. I explained I was taking hot water for Miss Nili. *'Sauna!'* I said cleverly.

'Where?'

When I told him, he took the pail from me and went out to where she was. She emerged and saw him. She opened the big dark blanket like the wings of a bird. 'Coming in?'

I couldn't see his face from where I was but I could see his shoulders stiffen. He poured the water in. 'Where did you learn to do this?'

She laughed. 'I needed the heat.'

'Do you know what the time is?'

She laughed again. 'Don't you even want to feel it, *darling*?'

*

TWO DECKS of playing-cards lay next to each other: one pack backed with a picture of a jaded princess on a Mogul bed, decorated in gold leaf, and the other with her gazing at a blue peacock while her attendants whispered among themselves. Red, blue and white chips were stacked in a small mahogany coffin.

The poker crowd rolled in at midday: Dias, Tippy, Gomes, Danton Chidambaram and Susil Gunawardene whose fingers were forever smoothing his greased hair, sharpening his profile. I had an ice-box full of beer at the back ready for them to drink until they were merry enough to tuck into lunch.

Susil, like Dias, was a generally happy man. 'So, how *men*? Feeling good?'

Tippy was already seated, 'Lucky, lucky. Today my fingers feel like they were kissed, caressed *machang* by good fortune.'

'Oh-oh no, *men*, misfortune, *machang*. For you today misfortune.' Dias whipped his ever-present newspaper out of his pocket. 'Capricorn, no?' He shook his head grimly. 'Bad news today for you. Bad on the cusp. Who is Virgo, the virgin?'

Nili looked up. 'That's me, sweetie.' She looked sleek after her sauna, and distant.

'Oh-oh. Keep low, Nili, keep low. I say, this is a bad day for all of you according to this horoscope. Ranjan? Pisces, no? You also are in for a bit of a stormy time.'

'So nobody on the up then?' Susil beamed.

'With no girls here today, who can be?' Tippy chuckled, 'except, that is, for our hostess with the mostest.'

'I thought you were the one with the mostest. The hottest anyway,' Nili retorted.

'Why? What do you mean?'

'Leo is OK.' Dias came between them.

'That's you, no?'

'Yes, me.'

'And the bugger who wrote that rubbish I suppose.' Danton sneered. He believed in nothing without evidence. 'What do you say, Gomes?'

'My friend Alphonso told me that sometimes the editor just writes the horoscope by rearranging what was written the previous month. Nobody realizes that it's all the same.' His big, flat, flabby cheeks quivered. 'Everybody just reads their own!'

I snapped the tops off three bottles of beer.

'All right, all right. These newspapers are a joke, but the real thing can't be laughed at.' Dias looked stern for a moment. 'I know from experience.'

Everybody laughed as if he had made a joke. 'So, what does your birth chart say about a bit of pokery?' Tippy poked him in the chest.

'I am serious. These things can be very informative. My friend once went to . . . '

'Not another one of your crackpot *friends*!'

'He discovered this fellow who lives in a cave down near Matara and does the most incredible birth charts in the world. You go to him with your time and place of birth, and he works out everything. He can tell you all about your past and your future. My friend's uncle was told about his mother's suicide, you know, which even he didn't know at the time! For sure. *And* he was told his son would do the same. *Terrible*, but you remember that case, no? That chap who used to work at that bank, chap who went loopy? Started eating the banknotes or something?'

In the kitchen I had put the earthenware pot in which I cooked the chickens into the sink and filled it with water for washing. Into the same water I poured away some left-over milk. As it entered the oily water inside the sunken pot, a beautiful milky way rose: a slow cloud of liquid smoke uncoiling and running along the clay creases and unfurling gently in a silent underwater burst of white. You would expect the mixture of oil, water and milk to be shapeless, but the whole thing moved in such a pre-ordained way, as if each drop had its future determined in itself, that the entire cloud was contained in the shape of the pot even though the water was everywhere and the sink was full. I waited for ages to see what would happen. Nothing happened. I made a cup of tea for myself and then when I looked back at the sink the white cloud had settled at the bottom like a jelly. In a cup of tea the cloud-burst of milk—evaporated and diluted—always quickly disappeared into the newly formed colour of light mud. But the sink water somehow slowed down the burst so much that nothing in the end changed. I worked out that it must be the chicken fat. Fat made all the difference, and I thought this was significant. I wanted to tell someone. It struck me that if a fluid could be so controlled in its apparently free fall, then why not our own lives?

The party was in full swing with a lot of loud laughing. Nili was arguing with Tippy and Mister Salgado. I looked around for Dias. He had distanced himself from the others and was studying the racing form.

'Sir, come and see this,' I said.

'Ah, Triton. What?' He looked bemused.

Then suddenly I realized that what I wanted to show him was almost impossible. It was something to do with myself, not simply oil and water. When he folded his paper and said, 'What is it?' again, I mumbled and tried to think of something else.

'The card-table. I put the India packs out. Is that right?'

'Why not, Triton?'

'I thought, with the star signs and all, you might want something special.'

He smiled benevolently. 'Good fellow,' he said. 'Good fellow. But whatever the pack, the fall of the cards is the thing. Now, what can you do about that?'

I shook my head helplessly. There is nothing you can do. Once my uncle took me to a friend's place. He was a *peon*. He had a khaki uniform and spent the whole day ferrying messages between two old men in two grey rooms who were endlessly adding and subtracting figures. But at night he played the cards. He would shuffle the pack for about thirty seconds, chanting all the time, then slam it down on the mat. He would then bet against my uncle simply on the colour of the card the pack would cut to: black or red. A week's wages on the turn of a colour. It was the fastest game in the world, he would say, and his eyes would gleam at the prospect of ruin in thirty seconds. They drank turpentine just to slow the game, because the more that was lost, the faster the shuffle. I was mesmerized by the snick and shuffle as much as the swift exchange of small fortunes. Cut!

Poker was a much slower affair. 'Sir, the cards fall as they will . . . ' I said.

Dias smiled, but before he could say anything, Tippy called out to him. 'I say, what does your astrologer say about the Beatles? Will they ever get back together? What, *men*, what?'

I had just started to put the food into dishes when the telephone rang. I answered; it was Robert. He wanted to speak to Nili. She came up behind me and I handed the receiver over. She didn't talk for very long; when she finished she went into her room. Next thing I knew, she was walking down to the gate. I went to her. 'What about lunch?'

She started to say something but changed her mind. Her eyes retreated, drying, even as she looked at me. 'If he asks, if he remembers, tell him I've gone out. Maybe I'll be back later, when they've finished playing . . .'

She asked me to fetch a taxi. Before she disappeared she told me, fiercely, 'Go feed them, Triton. Stuff their mouths and stop their stupid talk if you can.' She was gripping her shiny black handbag hard.

After she left, I finished my preparations and put the food out on the table buffet-style. Tippy could be relied on to make a start, and the others would follow suit. They would pile their plates high with mountains of rice and big pools of chicken curry, and then find a perch where they could fill their bellies and suck the marrow out of every bone until someone bullied them into playing cards.

'I say, where is Nili, *men*?' Susil asked.

Mister Salgado looked around, puzzled. I told him what had happened.

Tippy, across on the other side of the table, had ears like an elephant.

'Is that Robert fellow still around?'

Mister Salgado nodded.

'Helluva fellow that guy is. Ivy League man or something, but you should hear the things he gets up to . . .'

Dias came over, twisting and cracking a chicken bone with his teeth. He sucked hard and loud. 'What's that?'

'Have you heard of this Robert fellow?'

'I know him. Why, he came for that dinner here, no? At Christmas.'

'Bugger gets everywhere. He goes down to the villages on the coast and plays merry hell,' Tippy said.

'Why? Why?'

'Moonlight sea-bathing with the local girls and all. Moonlight . . . and nothing else, you know. He hands out loads of money to these village wenches and gets them to fornicate on the beach . . . '

'Don't talk nonsense. How can anyone do that?'

'Why *men*, you don't know how?'

'But he'll be stoned by our fellows, no? And chased off, surely?'

'More likely stoned out of his head.'

Tippy nudged Mister Salgado, 'Anyway, I hear he's moved into the Sea Hopper. Good job your Nili has stopped working there. She'd better keep her distance, huh? Ranjan?'

There was some more laughter. 'But I thought it was all *free love* in America, huh Tippy? Isn't that what you said? When you went to California and all that . . . ' Susil held his hands out in front of him and wiggled his fingers.

'There is no such thing as a free fuck,' someone muttered behind me. It was the infamous Pando of the chilli-bath, teetering with a large white hanky over his mouth. He still lived opposite us at number eight, alone, and sometimes when he noticed a crowd at our place, he would come over for a free meal and a beer.

'You should know, *machang*!'

Mister Salgado listened, turning an empty plate in his hands. I went and pulled him to the table. 'Take, Sir, food's getting cold,' I said. I put some rice on his plate and found a nice, firm thigh-piece for him with at least a little bit of flesh on it. 'Puppadum?'

He nodded and took a big, blistery one.

'Sir, sit over there.'

He went to one of the wooden chairs by the wall and sat down. His face was long, and his mouth was turned down at the corners. I left him to eat, or whatever, and got on with replenishing the dishes and getting more beer out. Without Nili the place was full only of men. 'I say, *machang*, pukka rice-puller no? Have you had?' Beer, rice and chicken curry: it was so easy to get them going. All except Mister Salgado who was gulping beer like a fish.

After the ice-cream, there was the inevitable chorus. 'Cards. Where are the cards? Bring the table, Triton.'

I pulled out the table. Tippy split the packs. Mister Salgado was hauled into the ring and given another beer.

'Banker, banker, let's have the chips.'

'Money first. Put your money where your mouth is.'

'Why? Nobody else in this bloody country does.'

'Like all these gurus, eh?' Danton grumbled. 'All fart and no shit.'

They made a big commotion of settling down to the game, partly to wake themselves up and partly out of a kind of weekend camaraderie. I took the food away and had a quick fistful or two of rice. Not much chicken was left, but I had kept back a couple of wings in the kitchen. With the card crowd, you could never count on having anything left over.

All afternoon there was no sign of Nili. I don't know

why I expected the telephone to ring with some message from her, but it never did. Mister Salgado was quiet, pre-occupied. Tippy regaled them with more stories of his travels in America. Susil, always on the lookout for a good deal, said, 'From what I hear we could do with a bit of this free-love business here. It might take the minds of these young thugs off their Marxist claptrap, huh?'

'But apparently in this new thing they are all joining, the dictum is no smoking, no drinking and no sex. Have you heard that?'

'What, *men*, not another monastery business? I thought they want a bloody revolution!'

Mister Salgado spoke. 'It's no joke you know. I heard even my chap down on the coast has started acting funny. He disappears off somewhere every month . . . '

'What rot, Ranjan. We are talking about a bunch of half-baked ruffians with nothing better to do. Your Wijetunga is an intelligent chap . . . Bugger has a job any-way, what's he got to complain about?'

Wijetunga's talk about the Five Lessons came back to me. A whiff of fermenting coconut husks. Two worlds spinning against each other.

'Not ruffians, *men*. What are you talking. Didn't you hear that election speech about hanging the losers by the balls? Skinning the bacon-eaters on Galle Face Green? That's us as well, you know. Not only the top dogs. And that fellow with all his threats will be in Parliament next month!'

'Rubbish. All talk. All these buggers want is a chance to put *their* hands in the honey-pot. Same as anybody.'

As the sun went down, I brewed a huge pot of tea for everyone. Tippy got up from the card-table. He had been drinking heavily. 'That's what we need!' he said to me in a loud voice. 'Pour the tea, *kolla*.' He didn't even look at me when I served him his cup. 'Dias, how come you are getting all these wild cards? What have you done? Stacked the pack or something?'

Mr Dias was smug. 'I told you: the stars are on my side today.'

'Bullshit.'

'Wait and see. I'll clean you out today.' He scooped up his chips and made a small pile of them.

'Double or quits?'

There was laughter all round except from Mister Salgado. He was staring at the little mound of chips on the other side of the table.

'What the hell is wrong with you, Ranjan?' Tippy asked. 'Not your lucky day?'

Mister Salgado looked at him morosely but said nothing.

I wanted to get away from all of them. Their talk. After serving the tea, I went out into the garden. With the sun down, the air moved gently as though the plants had begun to breathe again having held their breath all day. The drone of insects rose like scent. It was the time of the day when flowers would fall from the trees, petals bouncing off the small branches and resting briefly on a lower leaf before being released to touch the earth and die. The ground itself giving a little as the heat of the sun left it. I went to the gate and looked down the lane. There were two people walking towards the main road. When I first came to Mister Salgado's house, I used to spend twilight down by the gate. From there I could see two lampposts between the shade trees on the main road; soon after the sun sank, a man would come on a bicycle balancing a ten-foot pole in one hand. The tip of the pole had a metal hook like a mahout's stick used for tickling and tugging an elephant's ear. With it he would click the switch in the metal box halfway up the lamppost and release a slow flow of gas that would ignite and gently whiten the night like a phosphorus star. Then our red dirt lane would twitch like a dancing tongue as lights were switched on from house to house to avert the darkness as it rushed across the earth.

I looked back at our house. There were clouds moving behind it. Enormous eyes of yellow light stared out of the front. I should have let the tats down by now but I had been dreaming too long outdoors. Loud guffaws and sharp calls bounced around inside the house before tumbling out into the darkness.

I heard Tippy call me, 'Triton, *kolla*, beer!' But I didn't go. If he wanted it so much he could fetch it himself. In any case, it was high time they all left. I waited in the shadows. Tippy called out for me again tapping a glass against a bottle. 'Four aces, beat that!' Dias shouted delightedly.

'Aiyo!' Somebody else slapped his thighs and flung down his cards.

Chips clattered. A bottle of beer was brought from the kitchen. 'I could find only one.' I heard the top snap open. Someone turned up the music: an electronic wail in a purple haze.

'Where the hell is that bugger, Triton?'

I shoved my arm in the air and swore at them under my breath. *Kiss the sky!* Something in the night air infected me too. Too much was going on. Wijetunga on the beach had worked it all out. I wished I *had* finished my school certificate. Stupid, stupid boy. Stupid *kolla*. I felt panic in my mouth. I saw Joseph with a poisoned skull in his hand, smeared with *bali* ash, grinning by the gate. He too seemed to be floating in the air. *Eat it, kolla, eat it.* Inside me, everything was burning up.

'That's it,' Tippy shouted. 'I quit.'

'Helluva fellow you are. Just because you are losing . . . '

Somebody scraped a chair on my polished floor; it felt like a knife tearing my skin. I crouched smooth as a leopard in the dark; the soles of my feet hurt. The rocks on the drive pressed in. The party was breaking up as if by some unconscious collective decision the game had reached its end. I saw Tippy draining a glass of beer.

In a slow clumsy dance the apish figures toppled out of the house and disappeared into their humpy, black cars. The motors coughed into life and they rolled on bloated tyres out on to the dark, quiet road. Things always seemed to come to an end surprisingly abruptly; then it was as if nothing had ever happened. It might all have been a dream.

Later, while I was still outside, Nili came back. Mister Salgado, slumped on the card-table, seemed unaware of her return.

I didn't want to clear up. I didn't want to intrude on Miss Nili and Mister Salgado. After a while I walked down to the main road. I watched the traffic go from nowhere to nowhere. I could feel the ocean pressing around us.

*

When I brought the tea the next morning I found Mister Salgado already up. He was sitting out on the veranda in his sarong, staring at the gate at the end of the drive. A small golden oriole swooped down from a tree and flew over the garden. Mister Salgado didn't notice it. He was like a statue: in repose, eyes slung low, cheeks flat and his mouth, his lips, weightless. It was as though nothing in this world, or the next, could ever stir him. He didn't even blink. I guessed he had not slept much despite the day-long binge.

'Sir, shall I pour tea?' The same old words as always, but that awkward night had changed everything.

He did not move. He stared straight ahead. I asked him again, 'Tea?'

Eventually, very slowly, he turned his head towards me. Nothing showed in his face; hardly a muscle seemed to shift. I took his acknowledgement as my instruction to pour. The tea came out of the spout in a thick brown torrent.

'*Nona?*' I asked.

He pretended not to hear me.

She would usually emerge soon after him, but this morning there was no sign of her. I looked at the white doors behind him leading to the bedroom. They were firmly shut, almost as though they had not been opened all morning.

In the night I had heard them from the lane. First I heard Nili shouting at him. Loud enough for the whole neighbourhood to cringe. I heard him only when I slipped in through the back door. His voice seemed to swell out of his whole body like a dam bursting. I had never heard him like that before; although Nili had lost her temper before, I had never heard *his* voice turn ugly. It was harsh. He accused her of going to bed with Robert. 'I saw you *shaping* for that swine.' I looked in through the back door which was slightly open. Her face was screwed up. The cords in her throat were taut. She was swallowing hard. 'How dare you . . . You think you are a fucking genius but you know fucking nothing. Your stupid friends piss in your head and your brains bloody melt out of your fucking prick. How dare you accuse me . . . ' She pushed a chair out of her way. It hit the standard lamp: the lamp fell. 'You know what you are? A stupid shit. A barbarian. Just like the rest of them. You think just because I sleep with you, you own me. You stupid *goof.*' It was only then that I realized how much I had moulded her in my imagination. How little I had seen of her, really. Now, after all these years, I can hardly picture her face, her whole face. Only details come back: her eyes, dimples, her mouth filled with cake, laughing, and then this anger spewing out of it. She stormed off. Mister Salgado stood in the middle of the room, disfigured by the beams of the fallen lamp. Eventually he bent down and picked up the lamp. I went to my room and shut the door hard.

The oriole came back. It had never come so close to the house before. I could see it behind Mister Salgado: tangerine yellow, a bold black head, bright red-ringed eyes, a red beak. It was small, and yet its voice could fill the whole garden; its yellow plumage like a lick of paint. It sang deadpan. No anguish. No fear of the eagle that would swoop down on it one day and rip its yellow feathers. In blissful ignorance it is completely beautiful; unruffled until its last moment, until it is too late.

'Sir,' I whispered to Mister Salgado. 'Look, the bird.'

He looked at it but still showed no emotion. He had once found me with a dead bird in my hand. It was in the early days, when I was a young boy in the house. I had made a catapult and was practising down by the gate, perfecting my aim so that I could knock down mangoes from Ravi's tree. A little bird flew down and perched on a branch above: the challenge was irresistible. My aim was better than I expected. It fell at the first shot. The small plump body flopped down on the drive like a cloth ball. When I picked it up, the feathers felt silky soft, the tiny bones fragile and crushable. It was still warm. Mister Salgado came out and found me with it in my hand. He held my wrist and said, 'You know, you must not take life. To destroy is easy, but you do not have the gift to make life so easily.' Shame filled every vein in my body. I wished I were dead.

In the bay room the card-table and chairs looked eerie, as though the players had suddenly evaporated. The smell of beer hung in the air. I should have cleared the glasses away in the night. They were full of insects, drunk and dead. I would have done, but knowing the two of them were in there, alone, playing whatever it was they were playing at, I could not go in. It was impossible.

Inside the house, in the dining-room, I found my *sambol* on the floor. The dish rolled under the dining-table. The lasagne I had made and kept in the fridge was on the table with a great, gaping hole in the middle where someone had scooped out a spoonful. My heart slipped in my chest. If they were hungry, I should have been there. I found a spoon by the lamp and meat sauce on the wall. My lasagne.

I had been so proud to show her how I made it. How

the dough had to be kneaded before being rolled out and cut into oblongs. Her fingernails traced the small ridges and irregularities of the pieces, and her fingers smoothed the surface. She was so close I could smell her hair. She said, 'You don't really belong here, Triton.' It was not what I felt. There was nowhere else I belonged. I didn't know what she meant. 'We've all been put in the wrong place. We will never really produce anything here,' she said and touched my face with her hand. 'Only our grotesque selves.' Her hand was soft with a light oily sheen. I wanted to kiss it. I felt the impossible rise inside me: to be anything but invisible. I think she knew it, and perhaps I should have, whatever the consequences. But I felt I was fading. She stroked my face as if she were rubbing me out. My cheek felt numb. I didn't know what was going on but whatever it was, it was going wrong. If there are gods in this world, or in the next, let them take pity on us and give us strength every day, because we need it every day. Every single day. There is no let-up, ever. Not really.

*

MISTER SALGADO hardly moved at all. I offered him everything—even wood-apple cream—but nothing interested him. He did not want anything. Nili was nowhere. I didn't dare go into the bedroom.

'Sir, a little water at least. This sun . . . ' But he didn't stir. He was completely lost inside himself. Steam rose from his head in the broad beams of the mid-morning sun, and the air around his seated figure rippled with his body heat like concentric after-images of himself as he shrank, shiver by shiver, into a dehydrated huddle.

I took up all the carpets and rugs and beat them out on the driveway until the whole place was enveloped in a dust storm; I polished the veranda floor and the sitting-room floor with coconut husks, rasping my way to and fro, up and down the whole place. I flushed the drains outside the bedroom with disinfectant; I even went up on the roof to clear the gutters and make a big noise to chase away the bandicoot. Mister Salgado did not budge. There was no reaction. I cleaned the whole place and pretended nothing was wrong. Pretended that it was a morning like any other, and that it would pass to noon, to afternoon, to evening and night. And that after sleep all would be well. The next day would bring comfort and respite from the wrongs of the day. But it did not. By afternoon I knew Nili had gone. She had left while I was out at the shop. She never even said goodbye. It was better like that. I would have found it too confusing.

The days passed. In the end I started to pretend people were visiting us, to try and get him interested in what might be happening. I opened the gate and made noises as if visitors were arriving. I started going about the house talking to myself, trying to stimulate a conversation out of thin air. But if he heard me, he did not show it. It was as if he were under a spell; the whole house was dark.

He appeared fixed to the one chair. It changed shape as if to accommodate his immobile figure. Although the back of the chair in its graceful S-curve followed his own long spine, the wickerwork had burst in places. A few loose, frayed cane strips quivered like small springs underneath. He had swung the swivel-arms out so that they extended a full leg-length, knock-kneed and splayed. He rested his feet on them. The colour of his skin was almost the same as the wood of the chair. His arm was like another piece of wood—a round pole—resting on top of the side of the chair. I waited for it to turn towards me, to beckon me, to reach out for me.

'Sir, eat something now. Sir, even mendicants eat,' I whispered softly. 'Nuts? Honey and curd?' I left a tray on the small jakwood table for him to take at his own speed.

*

VESAK THAT year came soon after Nili left, a week before the Elections. Timely. A celebration of the birth of Buddha and his enlightenment—non-attachment—was exactly what we, in our house, needed. I wanted to make the biggest cluster of *vesak-kudu* lanterns ever seen in our irregular lane. I thought we might get some merit from doing that. The Lord knows we needed it.

I did it outside the kitchen. Mister Salgado didn't bother coming back there, even though I would have liked to have shown him what I was doing: the intricacies of the bamboo work, the splints, the knots, the magic by which an extraordinary structure of hexagons would appear, like his precious corals, out of nowhere, and link up with each other to become a brood of floating lanterns with long sea-trails of gossamer ribbons. I used white and Buddhist yellow tissue, rice for glue and white twine for binding. By the time I had the whole cluster done, my back ached but I was happy.

I fitted a rope on to the big white tree in the front and hoisted up the big mother with its six baby lanterns, all with candles lit inside.

'Sir, come and look,' I called him when it was up. He came. He stood on the steps and looked up. The light from the candles fell on his face. I pointed out the cascade of streamers. 'Look, I made them full-length.'

'Good,' he said.

Later that night I found him staring at the moon kicked high above the temple trees. 'If only we could make the whole coast like Yala. A sea sanctuary, with not a soul there. A real refuge.' He turned and looked hard at me. 'I can see it like a dream, you know, painted in my head.'

'Sir?'

'But the trouble is all these people. People who want to live just for today. Let tomorrow take care of itself, as if nothing ever matters but their own moment of passion.' He lowered his troubled eyelids. 'The thing you have to learn is to let what will happen, happen, I suppose. Not to struggle, not for anything.'

The next morning I asked him whether he would like an egg-flip for breakfast: my own mixture of high-grown coffee, cocoa, raw egg, vanilla and brandy whisked with hot milk and butter and stirred with a cinnamon stick; sprinkled with ground nutmeg—nutritious and delicious.

'No.'

I made the egg-flip anyway and offered it again later in the morning. When he refused it a second time, I drank it myself.

*

THE GENERAL Election that month resulted in a landslide victory for the opposition parties, an uneasy coalition of old-fashioned leftists and new-style nationalists who promised free rice and a new society; we were to be freed from market exploitation and liberated from the doom of a colonial inheritance. There were furious debates about the shape of the future: an epoch of water, power and resettlement, exaggerated visions of territorial politicians. In the spasm of change that convulsed the administration, Dias was posted to a job in the deep south. He came and told Mister Salgado the news. 'Everything is buzzing, *men!*'

'When do you go?'

'Next week.' He blew a perfect ring of Gold Leaf smoke. 'Doesn't look good for your coral business, you know. No more highfalutin ideas. It's all People's Committees now. That's decreed.'

Mister Salgado nodded. 'I know. People think they can rule even the waves by decree.'

'But we need the change. It's been topsy-turvy too long, Ranjan. Only thing, I don't know what I can do in this new system. Where I fit in.' Dias rubbed his eyes vigorously with both hands. 'What about you? What are you going to do?'

'I don't know.' Mister Salgado shrugged. After a moment he took a deep breath and lowered his head. 'I made a big mistake, you know,' he said. 'A big, big mistake.'

'Why don't you call her then? Try something.'

'I can't. I don't know where she is.'

'The hotel?'

'No, I think she's gone away.' He shook his head. 'Anyway, I don't really want to . . .'

'Only people with money are leaving. For England,

Australia. The classic flight of capital.'

'Good riddance, you mean.'

In the fading light they looked as they used to long before, lazing in our cool bay-room with the tats rolled up; but that evening there was no sound of laughter to fill the spaces between their lonely words.

*

MAYBE IT was not just us; maybe the whole world was changing. Over the next couple of months it seemed small wars, squabbles and a hunger for violence took grip everywhere: Belfast, Phnom Penh, Amman, places I had never heard of before, as well as our own small provinces. The *takarang* tank collapsed, the driveway flooded. Across the road Mr Pando rigged a roll of barbed wire along the top of his boundary wall, while his neighbours started to construct an apartment block in the front garden to house their children's quarrelling families. The older houses would all be eclipsed by the premium on land, the reformed regulations. Even ours, I could see, would one day have to give way and disappear behind a façade of somebody else's concrete. Our walls would crumble. The whole geography of our past would be reconstructed. It seemed nothing could remain the same.

One evening Mister Salgado came into the kitchen. He peered around like a stranger. 'I was trying to remember the *Anguli-maala* story?' he said looking at my hands.

'The sermon?'

'What went wrong? Was the prince mad or what?' Mister Salgado couldn't tell pork from chicken any more. He was still in a daze.

Anguli-maala is the story of Prince Ahimsaka the harmless. A bright young man who was devoted to his studies in a world full of envy. It was a bad time. All the other princes hated him. They told vicious stories about him, they spread ugly rumours. They told his teachers that he was having an affair with the headmaster's wife. The maddened headmaster decided to punish him by casting him into a hell of his own making. The prince was told that he must go out into the world and collect a thousand bleeding little fingers in a garland, in order to complete his studies. Today I suppose it might have been a thousand penises, but we little boys were told that it was fingers, little fingers. The prince reluctantly set off to do the bidding of his teacher and attain the promised wisdom by killing or maiming every man he came across; cutting off each little finger and threading a length of white cotton through the mutilated piece of flesh. Sometimes he just cut off the hand with his sword, other times he would chop the head off and then dismember the body, taking the finger. Through his loyalty to his teachers this once good prince became a mass murderer and grew to love the daily blood-letting. 'I am unable to sleep, I don't feel content until I have chopped ten little fingers,' he would say like a commandant to the ever-hungry cronies who gathered around him. 'I need the smell of fresh blood to breathe.' Then, when he had a nine hundred and ninety-nine fingers strung in a garland around his neck, he found the first fingers rotting and dropping like shrivelled hands of purple bananas. The stench was nauseating. The remaining fingers shrank and tightened around his throat. Sometimes he would dream of eating these fingers and wake up vomiting. He had to kill more and more, but could never reach his goal. Each time he threaded a new bleeding finger, ten old ones fell apart. But he did not stop. He said he had to do it for the good of the world, to become a wise and righteous king and sit on a golden throne. Down on the beach, the bodies of men and boys who had disappeared from their homes, who had been slaughtered by him and thrown in the sea, were washed in by the tide. Every morning they reappeared by the dozen: bloated and disfigured, rolling in the surf. The fishermen in the villages became undertakers. They burned heaps of the dead in bigger mounds than the fish they caught. Sometimes he would bury the corpses in mass graves, but the sea would unearth them, and the putrid flesh would be displayed on the sand, glistening, while crows picked at the pieces. Occasionally a body would be recognized and there would be whispers, relayed from mouth to mouth along the sea-paths up on to the highway and then along the treetops to all the villages up and down the coast. But there was no outcry. Only hushed incomprehension, terror or complicity. The earth and the sand, the sun and the wind, the sea and the dirty blue sky would temporarily hide the past, like the future, from the eyes of the world while the killing and maiming went on, faster and faster. This was punishment for whom? I used to wonder but I never asked; I could not make a sound under the nursery spell of the tale.

Mister Salgado watched my lips like a little boy, listening to me.

'Eventually the Lord Buddha heard these whispers and came to see what had happened to this once so devoted prince. And the prince who had turned into a monster recognized the Lord and realized the error of his ways . . . '

I was getting to the point where in my version it all ends happily and *Anguli-maala* becomes one of the most revered monks of all time, whose presence alone relieved the suffering of birth and brought peace to the living, but Mister Salgado had turned away. He shook himself in a deliberate shiver, like a dog, and retreated to his room. I didn't know it then, but earlier that day he had been told that Dias had disappeared. The report assumed he had drowned off the reef down south. A bad sea, it said, although I had never known Dias keen to go in even when it was calm.

It was only much later in the night that Mister Salgado could bring himself to tell me the news. His voice was barely audible. I could not believe we would never see Dias again. I felt sick: the thought of him tossed in the sea; fish darting through his unravelling self. The turbid water.

*

A Thousand Fingers

Towards the end of the year, Mister Salgado became restless. He moved from room to room in the house as if looking for something. He never seemed to find it. Nobody visited us. The old crowd disappeared. After the death of Dias, all our lives appeared to have changed irrevocably. But I could feel something in the air, as though we were in limbo. Treading water.

The first I heard of Mister Salgado's plan was when he came and told me, 'Triton, we are going away. Abroad. You must pack. Pack only what we need.' He made it seem simple. He explained that he had a job to go to at an institute in England. Something to do with his friend Professor Dunstable. He said I should go with him, fly to England. Maybe I too would be able to study; learn something and make a real life for myself. He meant we were leaving our house forever. It seemed the only way for him to be free of the gloom that had settled over him; over both of us.

I spent most of the rest of the day out in the garden close to our trees. The old white flame tree, the temple trees, the jam tree. But in the end I did as I was told, as always, and packed dozens of aromatic tea-chests with our belongings. There was no telling what we might need. I wanted to take everything, but Mister Salgado said we had to choose. I wondered who would come to live in the house after us: what sort of a world would they build on our remains?

Before we left, Mister Salgado showed me some photographs from his student days in England: a snowman with a hat, a crowd of grey greatcoats. 'It will be cold,' he warned. 'Ice and snow.' The prospect made me giddy.

'OK,' I said and stuck my thumb up as I had seen real heroes do in their flying machines on our panoramic Liberty screen.

IV

STRANDLINE

IN LONDON, MISTER Salgado settled us into an apartment near Gloucester Road and immediately started work at his institute. It rained continuously in those first months, dribbling down the sides of the building and darkening the wintry sky. The rain seemed to denude the trees and shrink the earth outside our window. I stayed indoors most of the time with the television on. Mister Salgado didn't have much time to show me anything. We didn't go anywhere until the following spring, when he arranged a visit to Wales where a colleague of his had a cottage to rent.

There was a pebble beach at the bottom of the cliff near the cottage. When the tide retreated, the shingle gave way to muddy sand and revealed the debris of a whole new world to me: Irish moss, moon jelly, sea kelp, razor-clams and cockle-shells, sand dollars and frisbees, blue nylon rope and dead sea urchins. In the evenings, when I walked along the path of crushed, purple-ringed mussel-shells and grey whelks, I would hear the sea birds cry, plaintive calls of cormorants and black-tipped herring-gulls as sad as our uprooted, overshadowed lives. Then the northern sun would find its prism and the sky would flare into an incandescent sunset above the oil refinery on the other side of the estuary; petrochemicals stained the air in mauve and pink as deliciously as the Tropic of Capricorn off our coral-spangled south coast back home. The sea shimmering between the black humps of barnacled rocks, mullioned with gold bladder-wrack like beached whales, thickened into a great beast reaching landward, snuffling and gurgling. The sky would redden, the earth redden, the sea redden. In pock-marked, marooned rock pools speckled hermit-crabs and rubbery, red sea anemones dug in; limpets and periwinkles and bubble weed held fast waiting for the tide. Thin, furry tongues flickered out of their lidded shells, casting for the slightest light in the eddies of cool water.

I asked Mister Salgado, 'Do all the oceans flow one into the other? Is it the same sea here as back home?'

'Maybe.' He shrugged. 'The earth has spun with its real stars under a beautiful blue robe ever since the beginning of time. Now as the coral disappears, there will be nothing but sea and we will all return to it.'

The sea in our loins. A tear-drop for an island. A spinning blue globule for a planet. Salt. A wound.

Back home that April, in 1971, the first of the insurgencies erupted in a frenzy of gunfire and small explosions. Bands of zealous young guerrillas roamed the villages and townships staking out their place in a crude unending cortège. Thousands were killed in the reprisals. The heart of a generation was forever cauterized. 'Our civilizations are so frail,' Mister Salgado said, reading the news reports of ghastly beheadings on the beach. But these were only precursors of the staggering brutality that came, wave after wave, in the decades that followed: the suffocating infernos, the burning necklaces, flaming molten rings of fire; the Reign of Terror, abductions, disappearances and the crimes of ideology; this suppurating ethnic war. The bodies would roll again and again in the surf, they would be washed in by the tide and be beached by the dozen. The lives of brothers, sisters, men and women, lovers, fathers and mothers and children would be blighted time and again, unremembered.

But as we walked up the sheep-hill together he would only say, 'She could have been here, you know. Plucking mushrooms out of the earth, or tying a knot in the long grass.' He would hold my arm and step over the puddles on the pewter rocks. 'Look at the bracken rippling between the heather. Here even the wind weeps.'

In our Victorian London home, I would simmer a packet of green flageolets soaked in cold water for six hours; I would wait for him to spill another sentence or two from his head and mark one day from the next.

His job at the institute proved short-lived. 'Another country running out of money,' he said, nurturing his own tight-lipped regression. Back home when he had told his assistants that the south-coast project had been suspended, Wijetunga had gone crazy. He had threatened to blow up the bungalow. 'We can do it,' he had shrieked, shaking a clenched fist. *No messing, boyo.* But here, when it came to his turn, Mister Salgado took the news as another simple fact of life. He found another, more modest job with a local education authority. 'It's not what you do every day, but the thoughts that you live with that matter,' he would tell me, tapping his head with his finger. 'That, after all, is the sum total of your life in the end.' I would light the gas fire in the sitting-room and bring out the beer.

'So, why did we come here then?' I asked. 'Like refugees?'

'We came to see and learn,' he said, parting the net curtains and staring out at a line of closely pollarded trees. 'Remember?'

But are we not all refugees from something? Whether we stay or go or return, we all need refuge from the world beyond our fingertips at some time. When I was asked by a woman at the pub, 'Have you come from Africa, away from that wicked Amin?' I said, 'No, I am an explorer on a voyage of discovery,' as I imagined my Mister Salgado would have replied. The smoke was thick and heavy like a cloud of yeast spread everywhere. She laughed, touching my arm and moving closer in the dark. A warm Shetland jumper. A slack but yielding skin with patchouli behind her ears. I was learning that human history is always a story of somebody's diaspora: a struggle between those who expel, repel or curtail—possess, divide and rule— and those who keep the flame alive from night to night, mouth to mouth, enlarging the world with each flick of a tongue.

Every May I brought out our summer clothes with their bygone labels—*Batik Boutique, CoolMan of Colpetty*—and replenished the spice-racks in the larder. I would try to imagine where I would be, and he, the coming winter when the snow might fall for Christmas and Norfolk turkeys would brown in native kitchens: we would move to yet another short-let property. Mister

Salgado's hair turned grey from the temples upward and he began to wear tinted spectacles. Finally, in '76, he said it was time to settle down. He bought a maisonette in Earls Court. There was a magnolia tree in the garden. We learned to sit silently in big, brown chairs and watch the creamy flowers peel, petal by petal, under a red sun sinking somewhere in Wiltshire.

I read all Mister Salgado's books, one by one, over the years. There must have been a thousand books in the sitting-room by the end, each a doorway leading somewhere I had never been before. And even after I had read all of them, each time I looked I would find something new. A play of light and shadow; something flitting in and out of a story I knew by heart. New books came every week. After years of tracking his books and after thousands of pages read and reread, I knew instinctively where he would put the newcomers, as if we had both attuned our own inner shelving to a common frame out of the things we read, separately, in our time together. We never spoke about it, but I am sure he also constructed a kind of syllabus for me to follow. He would leave particular books in particular places: on the toilet roll or on top of a pile of his clothes or balanced precariously on the edge of a table with a teacup on top, knowing I would tidy them away and, as I did so, would dip in and be captivated: *The Wishing Well, Ginipettiya, The Island.* I am sure he wanted me to read these books, but I don't know whether he knew that I read all his other books as well; all his boxed but boundless realities.

I went to classes and other libraries, night and day, for almost all the years we spent in London together; broke all the old taboos and slowly freed myself from the demons of our past: what is over is over forever, I thought.

'Why is it so much less frightening here,' I asked him, 'even on the darkest night?'

'It's your imagination,' he said. 'It is not yet poisoned in this place.' As if we each had an inner threshold that had to be breached before our surroundings could torment us.

One day I showed him a newspaper report about a symposium on Man and Coral that had taken place. 'You should have been there,' I said. 'Presiding over it all.'

He looked wistful. 'It was a kind of obsession before, you know.'

'But other people now, at last, all over the world seem to share that obsession . . . '

'You remember, all one ocean, no? The debris of one mind floats to another. The same little polyp grows the idea in another head.' He smiled and touched my head. 'But these gatherings are full of people who see the world in a different way now. They carry a lot of heavy equipment, you know. Suntan oil. Scuba tanks. They are only concerned with the how, not the why. I belong to another world. Even Darwin searched his desk for a pen, more than the seabed, you know. He relied on reports, talk, gossip. A tallowline. He looked into himself. In our minds we have swum in the same sea. Do you understand? An imagined world.'

The one time I did swim out to Mister Salgado's real reef, back home, I was frightened by its exuberance. The shallow water seethed with creatures. Flickering eyes, whirling tails, fish of a hundred colours darting and digging, sea snakes, sea-slugs, tentacles sprouting and grasping everywhere. It was a jungle of writhing shapes, magnified and distorted, growing at every move, looming out of the unknown, startling in its hidden brilliance. Suspended in the most primal of sensations, I slowly began to see that everything was perpetually devouring its surroundings. I swam into a sea of sound; my hoarse breathing suddenly punctuated by clicking and clattering, the crunching of fish feeding on the white tips of golden staghorn. My own fingertips seemed to whiten before me as trigger-fish, angel-fish, tiger-fish, tetrons, electrons and sandstone puffer-fish swirled around me, ever hungry.

Mister Salgado shook his head. 'I should have done something of my own with that bay. I used to think that in a month or two, the next year, I would have a chance to turn the whole bay into a sanctuary. A marine park. I used to plan it in my head: how I'd build a jetty, a safe marina for little blue glass-bottomed boats, some outriggers with red sails, and then a sort of floating restaurant at one end. You could have produced your finest chilli crab there, you know, and the best stuffed sea-cucumbers. Just think of it: a row of silver tureens with red crab-claws in black bean sauce, yellow rice and squid in red wine, a roasted red snapper as big as your arm, shark fin and fried seaweed. It would have been a temple to your gastronomic god, no? I thought of it like a ring, a circular platform with the sea in the middle. We could have farmed for the table and nurtured rare breeds for the wild. A centre to study our pre-history. We could have shown the world something then, something really fabulous. What a waste.'

'Let's do it here,' I said. 'Let's open a restaurant here, in London.'

'That's for you to do,' he said. 'Some day, for yourself.'

He bought the red Volkswagen about that time and

taught me to drive. We motored all over the country. We would fill up the tank on a Sunday morning and drive for miles visiting every historic house, garden, park and museum within a day's circuit. 'The Cook's Tour' he called it with a happy smile, and everywhere explained to me the origins of each artefact we came across. 'The urge to build, to transform nature, to make something out of nothing is universal. But to conserve, to protect, to care for the past is something we have to learn,' he would say.

One cold, wet afternoon we came back to discover a small snack-bar at the end of our road up for sale. Mister Salgado said, 'Here's your chance. Make it come true.' He invested the last of his savings in it. I painted it the colours of our tropical sea. Bought some wicker chairs and a blackboard for the menu. I put coloured lights outside and bucket lanterns inside. It was ready to grow. Mister Salgado beamed.

Then, in the summer of 1983, mobs went on the rampage in Colombo. We saw pictures of young men, who looked no different from me, going berserk on what could have been our main road. The rampant violence made the television news night after night for weeks. There had been nothing like it when trouble had broken out before, when books had been burned and the first skirmishes had started. Even during the insurgency of '71, the news had come only in drifts, distanced. But this time images of cruelty, the birth of a war, flickered on the screens across the world as it happened. I remembered my fervent schoolmaster: his wobbly, black bicycle with its rust-eaten chain-guard, the schoolbook he always carried with him and the black umbrella that would bloom in the warm rain. I had found him in a ditch on the edge of our ricefield, that unsettled month which ended with me coming to Mister Salgado's house. His legs had been broken by a bunch of older boys who used to huddle in a hut in the schoolyard and chant the slogans of a shrinking world.

At the end of the summer, out of the blue one day, Tippy telephoned Mister Salgado. He was changing planes at Heathrow, heading for New York to do some deal. He said he got our number from Directory Enquiries; Tippy knew how things worked all over the world. He said it was wartime now, back home. 'Buggers are playing hell.' He talked about the political shenanigans, the posturing and the big money that was there to be made as always out of big trouble. 'Big bucks, boy,' he said. 'Big bloody bucks.' Right at the end he mentioned Nili. He said she was in a sanatorium off the Galle Road. She was on her own. The business with Robert had ended soon after we had left. He had gone back to the States. Eventually she had started a venture of her own: a guest house for tourists. It had done well. But then during the violence of the summer, a mob had been tipped off that Danton Chidambaram and another Tamil family had been given shelter there by Nili. Their own homes had been gutted. She had hidden the two families upstairs and scolded the louts who came after them. The next night a mob had come with cans of kerosene and set fire to the place. There had been wild dancing in the street. She went to pieces. 'In a mess, *men*. Hopeless. You know how it is, *muchang* . . . killing herself now. She has no one, really.'

Mister Salgado put the phone down and pressed his fingers to his temples. He repeated what Tippy had said to him. He told me he had to go and see her. 'I must go back.'

I had once asked her advice about a dish I was making.

She had shrugged her shoulders and said, 'You are the master now, the master of cooking!' I didn't tell my Mister Salgado that. Instead I said, 'It's been too many years. So much has happened.' I modelled my voice on his as I had always wanted to, but I knew I could not stop him. I should not.

'You know, Triton,' he said at the end, 'we are only what we remember, nothing more . . . all we have is the memory of what we have done or not done; whom we might have touched, even for a moment . . . ' His eyes were swollen with folds of dark skin under and over each eye. I knew he was going to leave me and he would never come back. I would remain and finally have to learn to live on my own. Only then did it dawn on me that this might be what I wanted deep down inside. What perhaps I had always wanted. The nights would be long at the Earls Court snack shop with its line of bedraggled, cosmopolitan itinerants. But they were the people I had to attend to: my future. My life would become a dream of musky hair, smoky bars and garish neon eyes. I would learn to talk and joke and entertain, to perfect the swagger of one who has found his vocation and, at last, a place to call his own. The snack shop would one day turn into a restaurant and I into a restaurateur. It was the only way I could succeed: without a past, without a name, without Ranjan Salgado standing by my side.

On a crisp cloudless Sunday morning I drove him to the airport. At the check-in counter, while searching for his ticket, he came across his spare keys. 'Here, you'd better have these,' he said and handed them to me. A couple of hours later he flew out, after a glimmer of hope in a far-away house of sorrow.